The Bravo Trail

ANOTHER SAGEBRUSH LARGE PRINT WESTERN BY
EUGENE CUNNINGHAM

Border Guns

The Bravo Trail

EUGENE CUNNINGHAM

Sagebrush
Large Print Westerns

Library of Congress Cataloging-in-Publication Data

Library of Congress CIP Data was not provided in time for publication. Please call (800) 818-7574 or (603) 772-1175 in the U.S. or Canada and we will fax or mail it to you.

Cataloguing in Publication Data is available from the British Library and the National Library of Australia.

Sagebrush Large Print Westerns are published in the United States and Canada by Thomas T. Beeler, Publisher, PO Box 659, Hampton Falls, New Hampshire 03844-0659. ISBN 1-57490-268-7

Published in the United Kingdom, Eire, and the Republic of South Africa by Isis Publishing Ltd., 7 Centremead, Osney Mead, Oxford OX2 0ES England. ISBN 0-7531-6252-0

Published in Australia and New Zealand by Bolinda Publishing Pty. Ltd., 17 Mohr Street, Tullamarine, 3043, Victoria, Australia. ISBN 1-74030-003-3

Manufactured by Sheridan Books in Chelsea, Michigan.

The Bravo Trail

CHAPTER 1

LACE MORROW TURNED VERY SLOWLY WHEN HE heard the big patrolman's heavy feet behind him in the stable doorway. He knew without looking that it was O'Connor. As he turned, it occurred to Lace that the San Francisco Police Department, in O'Connor's person, was showing too much interest in a livery-stable roustabout. But his square, red-brown face betrayed nothing of his feelings as he faced the big policeman. His hands hung limp at his sides—as if no effort of will power were required to keep his right hand from jumping up to the open throat of his shabby blue shirt, and sliding inside to whip the short-barreled .45 from the spring holster under his arm.

"Hello, Chief," he greeted the patrolman. "*Como le va?* How's it going?"

O'Connor's small, shrewd eyes seemed to probe Lace's blank features. Lace wondered just what thoughts were moving behind that pink face. For perhaps the twentieth time in two weeks, he studied the big, taciturn officer. Did O'Connor suspect him?

It was a long way to Pluma, that unimportant Southwestern county seat. But "fliers" on wanted bank-robbers—particularly when they carried notice of a thousand dollars reward—had a way of circulating to faraway places, of being read carefully. O'Connor might guess that he was looking at what amounted to a walking sight draft for a thousand dollars, and, if he did, some sort of blazing action could be expected. On the other hand, he was a good cop, so his daily pauses at this outlying stable might be caused by no more than

1

routine interest in any drifting roustabout who settled on the O'Connor beat.

The short Colt in the shoulder holster chafed Lace a little. He shifted his position. O'Connor, still looking at him, saw a man no more than five-nine, tremendously muscled, with hair and eyebrows bleached by years of sun almost to the color of tow.

He stared at O'Connor, and at the corners of his ice-blue eyes the tiny wrinkles—that testified to many hours of squinting into desert glare—deepened. Almost amusedly, he looked at O'Connor's long blue coat. Under it was hidden the patrolman's pistol. Lace wondered just what the mechanics of this situation would be, if O'Connor really suspected him.

He was a fearless officer, and one of the best shots on the San Francisco force. Only three months before, according to the story told by Dyce, the admiring livery-stable owner, O'Connor had walked into the little branch bank four blocks away—walked right into the middle of a hold-up. Very efficiently, he had shot two of the robbers and wounded the third so seriously that it was doubtful if he would ever come to trial. And yet—

"O'Connor," Lace said mentally, "if you started to reach under that coat of yours, to get out that six-shooter, and I wanted to kill you, I would have five slugs in your liver before your hand had moved six inches!"

"And what was the name of the tune I heard you whistling when I come along?" O'Connor inquired. He smiled genially at Lace. "Seems to me you're forever a-whistling of it."

"Oh, that!" Lace shrugged. "It's one I learned when I was a kid in Mexico. They call it *The Zebra Dun*. It's a good song, too. All about not taking a man for his face

2

value. The last verse of it runs:

> "There's one thing, and a sure thing,
> I've learned since I was born:
> Every educated fellow
> Ain't a plumb greenhorn!"

"And that's good sense, too, now," O'Connor nodded. "It's like that in police work. If you was to take every man for what he might be looking like in the face of him, a cop'd just as well be like them police I've heard about, down in South America, that puts down a lantern on the sidewalks of nights, then sets by it, so the crooks'll not be coming around doing burglaries and the like where a policeman'd be bothered by seeing 'em!"

Lace stared at him. Now, was this big Mick playing games with Lace Morrow? Was he saying something, and grinning within himself, because more was behind the words than appeared? Lace could hardly think so. O'Connor would never qualify for one of the world's bright minds. He was far more the bulldog than the fox.

But, just the same, there was something in the air that worried Lace. He had been "on the dodge" since his eighteenth year, and he was twenty-eight now. For ten years his freedom had depended upon smelling danger on the breeze, and beating the other man to the draw. These necessities had made him as instinctively alert by day or night as any ancient gray wolf of the Pluma Hills.

And for nine years of those ten his instincts and abilities had kept him as free as any ranging *lobo*, for all that Sheriff Jacks of Pluma could do. Until, through the treachery of a man he had considered his friend, Jacks had taken him asleep under that man's roof.

Took me, but couldn't hold me, Lace thought, now

3

with a little grim amusement. Took me and stood me up in the district court room to stand trial, convicted me of bank-robbing, started to the penitentiary with me—but he couldn't make it!

He had caught the little sheriff off guard and tied him with his own belt in a pullman berth, then jumped from the racing train, escaping twenty years in Huntsville.

He moved wide shoulders restlessly. It might be no more than natural tension, with final escape so near. Down near Islais Creek on the waterfront, he had passage booked on the rusty little *Negrito*. The tramp would sail for South American ports within three or four days. And once out on the Pacific, Lace Morrow would never trouble himself again about Sheriff Jacks. In the Argentine he would forget Pluma, forget the Southwest, wipe out of his memory all the searing details of his forced outlawry.

He moved away from O'Connor, saying over his shoulder, "Got to be cleaning up the stalls."

He pulled the old cap over his forehead and looked down at himself, at the faded blue shirt and dirty overalls and heavy-soled shoes—worn on feet which had always been shod, in the days of his cowpuncherdom, with nothing less than the finest bench-made boots.

"What would I want to think O'Connor'd suspect me for?" he asked himself sardonically. "Men who knew me well would hardly see Dandy Lace Morrow in this rig! I'm just skittish for nothing, I reckon. Once I'm out Golden Gate, I'll be long gone from the old places. I'll never ride the high lines again. Never no more . . ."

He passed his employer inside the stable. It seemed to Lace that Dyce looked at him with an odd intentness—

and then an instant later put on an air that was equally peculiar, of not being interested in him at all. Lace thought of this as he picked up his shovel and stepped into the first stall.

Once sheltered by its half-wall, he turned. A low mutter of voices carried to him. He looked out. O'Connor and Dyce stood near the office with their heads close together. After a moment O'Connor nodded and went into the office. Lace leaned a trifle and saw the big patrolman standing with the telephone in his hands. Dyce was watching with strain in his manner.

Lace nodded grimly. So he *was* suspicious of me! That's the why of all the smooth little questions he's been asking, this last week or more. Well, thanks be! Nobody can hook Roustabout Jones to the fellow that booked on the *Negrito*. All I've got to do is slide down into one of those waterfront boarding houses and lay low until the tramp sails. None of the police are likely to uncover me, either!

He grinned tightly and began to move down the line of stalls. Right here, right now, is where one top hand makes him a great big hole, in the Frisco fog!

In the last stall of the row, he stopped with head thrust forward, his wide, thin mouth a little open, his blue eyes very narrow. He heard the footsteps of several men, heavy and slow and cautious footsteps.

"So you really made me, O'Connor, did you?" Lace whispered. "You really made me—and didn't let your face show it . . ."

For three big men in plain clothes now stood by the office door. Dyce was with them. The livery-stable owner was telling them something in an undertone that carried the distance to Lace Morrow only as a harsh murmur.

Lace grinned ironically, made a little contemptuous salute to them, and whispered, "Be seeing you! Yeh— be seeing you, if I bodaciously can't keep from doing that li'l thing."

Then he went with hardly more noise than a snake might have made, over the half-wall of the stall, and past three horses. Out of the last stall he slipped into a dark harness room at the end of the big stable. He barred the door behind him and opened the window silently. He had tested that window time after time by way of forethoughted maneuver. He could get through it and into the yard directly below without alarming the keenest ears outside the stall.

That yard was behind an apartment house which fronted on the next avenue. When Lace dropped to its smooth, green sod, a woman thrust her head out of a first-floor window. She was a big woman, red-faced, with a suspicious expression. Lace put a hand to his shabby cap and smiled upon her.

"And what do you think you might be doing?" she demanded angrily. "Running over me grass and me flowers that takes hours and hours of me time and—"

"I'm after one of our horses, ma'am," Lace told her quickly, for her voice threatened to carry even into the stable. "A bad horse that broke loose. If you don't mind me cutting through your yard, I can head him off. I wouldn't want him trampling your flowers and grass and scaring the children—"

"Oh!" Her voice dropped by many notes. She nodded. "Sure, if it's a loose harse, you run right through to the street. The quicker you catch him the better, with the children loose like so many harses themselves—"

He ran on into the roofed passage that led to the avenue. He opened the door of this tradesmen's entry and looked up and down. No sign of policemen and—it seemed providential to Lace—a baker's wagon came clattering toward him, headed toward the Park. Lace streaked out into the street and swung up to the round, iron step of the wagon. He grinned at the driver, a freckled youth of round, innocent face.

"Give me a lift as far as Fulton, will you? I'm from the stable back there. One of our horses broke loose. Got to round him up. He's a hard-mouthed brute and it's a wonder he don't murder some of these fancy riders. I swear! What they don't know about horses! If you want to know which way they're going you've got to ask the horse."

"Help yourself," the boy said, grinning. "Yeh, they're dumb."

CHAPTER 2

LACE AND THE FRECKLED DRIVER TALKED HORSES until the wagon reached Fulton Street. Lace looked with elaborate care up and down the street and shook his head. He dropped off.

"Must have got inside the Park," he said. "Thanks a lot, Mister. You really don't know how much I appreciate the lift."

He ran across the width of Fulton and into the Park. He cut through brush to a bridleway and walked along it fast. No pursuit showed behind him. He headed toward that patch of thick trees where his wooden box was hidden. Before reaching there he had slipped aside into undergrowth three times, at the sound of someone approaching.

Reckon there's no particular hurry, he thought.

Likely, O'Connor telephoned to that posse of his, and had'em ambushed somewhere close around. He came on ahead to see that I was waiting to collect the jewelry, then telephoned for'em to come pin the tag on me. And they can't be sure I headed for the Park—not unless they should run into that cake-wagon boy.

He heard the thud of hoofs on the path behind him and slid to the side, going behind a tree to crouch. It was a mounted policeman cantering toward him. But the officer seemed to have nothing special in mind. He passed and Lace straightened. Leaves cracked on the ground to the left.

"Grab your ears, Lace!" a familiar voice commanded. "You know I'll cut you in two if I have to . . ."

Lace jerked his hands upward without hesitation. Roy Jacks was hardly likely to feel kindly toward the man who had left him strapped to a pullman berth for the world to find . . . And he was quite as good a shot, if not so fast on the draw, as even Lace Morrow.

"You're the doctor!" he told Pluma County's sheriff calmly. "But, I swear! I didn't expect you to come popping out like this. I thought I was just dealing with a bunch of pilgrims."

"You would have fooled 'em, too," Jacks drawled from directly behind him. "I told 'em you would naturally be around hawses, somewheres. So we figured out how many riding academies and stables and all there was in Frisco, and talked to the po-licemen in those neighborhoods. Fella named O'Connor was a-watching you, anyhow. So, it wasn't hard. And when they started making up their posse to take you in, I had a notion you might hoodle 'em. And if you got clear, you'd head this way. And, by Gemini! That's just what you done."

"I always said you're a better sheriff than Pluma folks

deserve, Roy," Lace told him courteously.

"Let your hands down slo-ow, behind you," the little sheriff instructed his prisoner. "I got the cuffs in my right hand—maybe you recollect I shoot a li'l bit better with my left . . ."

Lace obeyed with deliberation. His hands came slowly down until both were behind him, at waist-level. But he did not stop the movement, then. His right hand twitched up, caught the barrel of Jacks' pistol and shoved it. He pivoted on a heel and his hard left fist, making a great loop, smashed into Roy Jacks' unguarded belly.

The sheriff grunted and doubled in agony. The pistol fell from his limp hand without exploding. Lace pounced upon him in a jaguar-swift leap, caught up the dropped handcuffs and snapped one over Jacks' right wrist. He took a hideout, a stubby .38, from under the sheriff's arm. Then, bodily, he lifted the smaller man and set him against a small tree. When he was done, Jacks was braceleted, hands behind him, to that slim, strong sapling.

Lace stepped back and regarded him with something like apology in his expression and his voice. "Dang it! I'm always having to get rough with you, Roy. I wish you'd give it up and let me lose myself. What are you always hounding me for? You ought to know they railroaded me for that bank job, just because I've been on the dodge so long. That bunch of detectives had to hang somebody, and I was handy."

"Long's I'm sheriff," Jacks told him gaspingly, "I'll keep after you till you hear Huntsville gates slam behind you. Then—Why'n't you listen to sense, Lace? This won't get you a thing. You can't head for the northern ranges and be free in your mind a minute. Somebody's

9

going to see a flier on you and make a play for that thousand the bank offered."

Lace laughed grimly. He had both of Jacks' Colts now, in his waistband. He worked his blue shirt over them. "You think so? There's a range I heard about, where all I'll need is a rimfire saddle, and to remember to dally my rope instead of tying. Nobody'll take me for a Texas man."

"You'll never make it out of Frisco," Jacks insisted. "I've got every po-liceman here on the lookout for you. And you won't kill an officer to keep from doing your twenty years. You know it and I know it. So you won't shoot your way out. Listen, Lace. You take these cuffs off me and come on back. Start in doing your time and look to getting a pardon after a few years. I can't help it if the jury found you guilty of something you never done. You better listen—"

"You must have misunderstood," Lace told him politely. "It was twenty years they handed me, Roy. Twenty years! Not six months on the chain gang. Pardon, you say? Blazes! The same record that got me the long stretch will keep any governor from pardoning me. I'll do the book and you dang well know I will."

Grimly, he stared at Jacks. "Twenty years. I'd be nearly fifty when I got out—not a bit of use for anything in the world. Twenty years behind Huntsville bars— almost as long as I've lived so far. And why? Because I was crowded into riding with the Smoky Hills gang when I was a kid. Because it's been said I had a hand in sticking up some trains and banks. Because I've rode the high lines. Because I was a Long Rider in a way. Because I have run some wet stock across the River."

He drew a long breath, looked quickly all around with wolfish alertness, relaxed again but with no lightening of his grim expression. Jacks shrugged. Before he could speak, Lace went on.

"When I quit all that and settled down, north of Pluma, nobody would let me alone. That was all I wanted—to be let alone to make a living off that one-cow place I bought. Tarnation! Do you think any man in his right mind wants to be on the dodge? I had ten years of it. I never did like it. And so I bought the Box M. And when the Darien bank was stuck up, you-all rode out to accuse me of staking out the job!"

"I never worked up the case against you. I never tried you," Roy Jacks told him calmly. "No use belly-aching about it, now, Lace. But you couldn't prove you never cased that job."

"You couldn't have proved you didn't, either! I was out on the range. Nobody saw me. I—But you're right. No use my belly-aching about it. But if you think I'm going back, if you think I can't get out of this town and make it north somewhere and start out—I'll make it to Canada if I have to. You'll work hard finding me there, or getting me out if you do!"

He laughed grimly and Roy Jacks, studying him nodded. "I see you're past talking to, Jacks admitted. "I know you won't go back and do your time, or such part as you have to."

Lace made a contemptuous sound. He leaned to take the little man's shirt out of his pants with a jerk. He tore it and unbuckled Jacks' waist belt. "Going to take your boots off, Roy. And your breeches. And I reckon I've got to wad your shirt-tail into your mouth. Your own fault, though! You're too dang good an officer."

He surveyed his finished work critically. Roy Jacks' grim, dark eyes went with him as he moved off, carrying pants and boots and pistols. At the edge of the thicket Lace turned to lift a hand in farewell. "I like you well enough, Roy. But I do hope I never put eyes on you again. *Adiós!*"

He hid the sheriff's possessions thoroughly, in several thick clumps of brush. Then, in the thicket where he had buried his box, he changed his clothes quickly. The outfit he put on was rough—such as merchant sailors buy for shore leave at the slop shops on the Embarcadero. When he was dressed he looked down at himself and grinned.

"Now, if nobody happens to run onto Roy in the next couple of hours, I'll be holed up down on East Street. And if I can't stay there a couple of days until the *Negrito* pulls out—"

He walked with caution through the Park until he came to its eastern end. Two policemen stood talking on Stanyan Street, but they hardly glanced at his slouching figure. He made California Street and swung onto the little cable-car. Dropping off at Market, to turn toward the waterfront, he grinned slightly.

"If they look for a cowboy in a sailor boarding house, we might just as well bust up the rules book and start over. That would be a little too much competition to buck!"

He got his room without a dozen words, in a rickety lodging house that faced the piers. And he sprawled upon the thin, hard mattress until the dirty windows grayed, considering what was best to do. He knew the saloon in which the *Negrito's* skipper passed his free hours. With dark, he would eat and find the thin-faced Italian and learn definitely when the tramp would sail. He would—

He had heard the ancient floor creak a dozen times outside his door, listened mechanically to the lurching

12

feet of sailors and longshoremen. But now it was as if some sixth sense had warned him that the tiny sound beyond that door was concerned with him. He came slowly, without noise, to his feet. The Colt was out of the shoulder holster in a deft, smooth movement. He looked about him.

Doors opened from this room to others. He went softly to one, found it locked, crossed with infinite pains to the other and tried the knob. The lock was stiff but he could push the latch away from the weak and twisted plate. He went into the adjoining room and closed the door behind him.

This was an empty room and his key fitted the hall door as it fitted his own. He unlocked that door and drew it to him. The hall was empty, for as far as he could see. There was no sound—until someone began rapping gently upon a door—upon the door of the room he had just left.

He pushed his shabby hat back and leaned a little until he could look into the hall, down at his own door. He saw the slim, stooping figure there and frowned. At least, it was not a policeman. Then the man turned and at the sight of his face Lace stiffened.

"By God!" he breathed to himself. "Judge Bettencourt! And what he'd be doing in Frisco, unless he came along with Jacks, I don't know . . ."

The slender man rapped again. And his low voice carried to Lace, even though the judge's lips were all but against the warped panel of the door—as if he wanted not to be overheard.

"Morrow! Oh, Morrow! This is Arnold Bettencourt. I want to talk to you. I have to talk to you!"

Lace Morrow's mouth tightened. He had left Roy Jacks cuffed to a tree; he would leave this judge who

13

had presided over his trial in Pluma, who had sentenced him to twenty years imprisonment, tied by his heels to the bed in there. And he would forget the *Negrito*; he would head north and in Oregon, perhaps in Canada, lose himself.

He slid into the hall and with pistol out moved like a puff of smoke toward the listening figure. "All right," he whispered, a yard from Bettencourt. "You can talk to me. But keep your voice away down. The first loud noise you make will be a death sentence *you* don't hand out."

Judge Bettencourt turned his gray head deliberately. He was clean-shaven, with a thin, aristocratic face. Now the only sign of life in his expression was in his eyes, large and so dark that in this gloomy hallway they were like pools of ink.

"I'm not armed, Morrow," he said quietly. "And I'm here to help you. That's going to be hard to believe—"

"Too hard," Lace said mockingly. "So I won't try it."

"You have to. This house is surrounded. By the police."

CHAPTER 3

LACE STARED GRIMLY, LISTENING FOR THE SOUND OF heavy feet on the creaking stair. A corner of his mouth lifted.

"Good advice," he said snarlingly. "I've had a lot of it lately. From Roy Jacks and from the good people of Pluma before today. 'Serve your time,' they told me. 'Get your sentence shortened by good behavior. Hope for a pardon.' And now you come up to tell me I'd better give myself up—"

14

"Oddly," Bettencourt's tone was almost humorous, "I'm telling you no such thing. I didn't come to San Francisco with Roy Jacks with any idea of helping capture you. I came here to find you for a reason there's no time, now, to discuss. You have got to get out of here quickly. I've looked the situation over and the only way to dodge the police is to go yonder, to the end of this hall. Go out that window and down a drain pipe to the left of it. There's a little passage under it. It will take you to the corner through a door at its end. Hurry! I tell you, what I want is to talk to you privately. Have you ever heard of Arnold Bettencourt breaking his word?"

Lace shook his head, frowning at the thin, pale face.

"Then I tell you, odd as it may seem to you now, I want nothing less than to see you recaptured and sent to Huntsville. I am helping a fugitive to escape—I, a district judge! Hurry! I'll wait for you at the corner of Market and Sacramento."

Perhaps it was the stealthy creaking of the stairs that made him resolve to trust Bettencourt, but Lace nodded shortly and ran, with no more noise than he had made stalking the judge, to the window indicated. He got it open with some difficulty, swung over the sill with pistol in his waistband and, after a quick look into the foggy well below, caught the drain pipe and worked down it to a cemented floor.

The passage was as Bettencourt had said. He went along it, around an elbow, and opened a door that gave upon the side street. The fog was thickening. Along the pier heads the Embarcadero's lights were misty yellow blobs in the darkness. An ideal night for him, Lace thought.

He went out and had taken perhaps a dozen steps when out of the shadows two burly figures lunged. A

15

match flared. Then a grim voice said, "And it's him, right enough! Want you young fellow—"

Lace whipped the pistol from his waistband and struck O'Connor across the side face. The other man—a big plain clothes officer—began to work at a pocket. Evidently, he had known little of the sort of man he came to catch, a creature as quick and savage of thought and movement as any wolf of the same plains which had bred Lace Morrow.

As O'Connor went down with the crash of a pole-axed bull, the detective staggered under Lace's second blow. With his hand still in his coat pocket upon the gun which should have been in his big paw from the beginning, he fell across the patrolman.

Somewhere toward Market Street a cable-car clanged in the misty darkness. Lace looked grimly down at the victims of his pistol—and their own excess of confidence. He listened briefly and looked along the street. But nobody moved. There was no sign that anyone had seen this quick exchange of blows.

He shackled O'Connor and the detective together, back to back, using the handcuffs of both. Then he went quickly along the sidewalk of East Street and up Market to the corner. Beyond the sign of The Magnolia Cafe an overcoated figure stood. Lace, with more thought of the puzzle Bettencourt presented than of the officers behind him, went up to the judge.

"Come on," Bettencourt said sharply. "If we meet anyone, I'll do the talking. We'll swing aboard the cable-car when it overtakes us. Right now, we want distance between us and the waterfront. Roy Jacks is nobody's fool. He evidently suspected you'd come this way, trying for a tramp steamer out of the country. And the fact that the police located you is proof of his brains.

16

But with a moderate amount of luck, he's seen his last of you *this* time . . ."

They moved rapidly. Presently, Bettencourt had to stop in a doorway, panting. Lace breathed only a little faster. He was hard as nails from his months of flight afoot, on stolen horses, on the rods of freight trains, and from the laborer-work he had done.

"Here's the car—and I don't see any suspicious passengers," Bettencourt sighed. "Let's catch it. I've a quiet apartment up the hill. Nobody will see us going in."

They caught the car and sat in silence until block after gray block of flats and apartments had been passed. When they dropped off, Bettencourt led the way around a corner and Lace, his hand on his pistol under the shabby sailor jersey he wore in lieu of a shirt, trailed him alertly. He followed into a dimly lit hallway and up a stairway. As he went he marked the ways by which he could escape if this should be a trap. And yet—his instinct did not warn him, now; he did not really believe himself in a trap.

When the judge unlocked a door and thrust it wide open, he entered without waiting for Lace. And Lace stood for a moment in the doorway, listening, looking. Then he came inside and shut the door after him. But he stood with his back to a wall for an instant, even after Bettencourt waved to a shabby, comfortable leather rocker.

He had known Arnold Bettencourt as a small boy, when the judge had been a young lawyer just out of college. But when Lace's father, Bowen Morrow, had been shot by horse-thieves, Lace had become a drifter, riding the chuckline up and down Texas, across Arizona and New Mexico and California, into Utah and down to

Old Mexico. He had neither seen nor heard of Bettencourt until his return to Pluma to buy the little Box M outfit. But Bowen Morrow had liked Bettencourt; he had always said that Bettencourt was that rare creature, a lawyer who looked at people more than at law books; a man whose word was as good as his bond. He crossed to the chair and sat down.

"Good," the judge said quietly. "For what I'm going to say to you is as odd as what has gone before—my helping you to get out of Roy Jacks' clutches. And if you can't believe me, and trust me, we'll get nowhere."

Lace studied the pale, clean-cut face for a time. Bettencourt stared past him at the window. "You're thinking that I'm the judge to whom you owe a sentence of twenty years. For a bank-robbery that—"

"—That I didn't have a thing to do with. Of course."

"The judge in such a case is not the jury, not in a district court. The prosecution made out a strong case against you. Whether you believe it or not, I watched to see that no unfair advantage was taken of you. And when the jury went out I asked myself if you were really guilty. To be perfectly honest with you, I rather thought you had got tired of the hard work on your poverty-stricken little ranch, and had listened to some old acquaintances. Your record was very much against you. So was the fact that you had money to pay extensive lawyers. I wasn't surprised when the jury brought back a verdict of guilty. I'm not apologizing in any way for the sentence I passed. It was neither inadequate nor excessive."

"For the things they found me guilty of," Lace admitted with a grim smile, "I reckon you're right; it averaged. But I didn't have a thing to do with the Darien job. I guessed who did stick up the bank. And maybe I

18

had a notion that some of the boys I'd rode high lines with made up a purse to pay my lawyers. We didn't bother much about where the money came from. It was dropped on the doorstep and we used it."

"Exactly! Now, since you broke arrest, I've heard things. Nothing to take into a court to furnish basis for a new trial, or reversal of that verdict. But enough to make me give you the benefit of the doubt. I'll go this far. If you tell me that you didn't help rob the Darien bank, I'll believe you. I might as well say that! I—have already told the Governor as much . . . Even argued the matter and won."

Lace leaned stiffly forward, frowning. "Won what?" he demanded, his tone puzzled.

"Won a proposition from the Governor, to be presented to you. If you accept it, I have a parole in my pocket. You can come back to Texas, free from any danger of arrest—"

"This is getting too much for me," Lace confessed. He shook his towy head. "You come out with Roy Jacks, knowing that he's on my trail. You've got a parole in your pocket, but you don't tell Jacks that. You let me crack two policemen over the head, to get clear of that rooming house, when all you'd have to do is show that parole—"

"I told you the whole affair is odd," Bettencourt reminded him. His mouth twitched humorously. "But the explanation of your puzzle is really very simple. First, you hadn't accepted the parole; haven't accepted it even now. So far as Jacks is concerned, you're still the escaped convict who tied him to a pullman berth and left him for the train crew to find. You know, young man, your habit of treating Jacks that way is highly disrespectful to the majesty of the law."

19

For the first time since meeting Bettencourt, Lace Morrow permitted himself a grin. "But think how that's practically going to be an education for Roy," he said. "I bet you the next time he starts to Huntsville with a long-stretcher, he'll watch that prisoner cross-eyed and antigodlin, every minute of the trip. A sheriff ought never to figure that because his prisoner is quiet, his prisoner is licked. But go ahead and let's hear the whys behind this parole business."

"In the beginning," Judge Bettencourt said gravely, "you do want to come back to Texas, don't you?"

"I don't know," Lace told him. "Considering that I've been spending a good deal of time getting as far away from Texas as I could, I reckon we could argue about that."

"I mean," the judge told him, "on a parole. A secret parole issued by the governor."

"What would he be paroling me for?" Lace demanded. And his eyes were hard and alert. "What would I get out of it? I'm free now."

"You are and I know of few men more likely to remain free. But if I read you aright, you don't want to stay on the dodge. You don't want to be an exile from your own country for the rest of your life. Suppose I offer you a chance to come back and do a certain favor, in payment for that parole?"

"Come on, judge! Come on, put your cards on the table! We're just going in circles," Lace said grimly. "Put your proposition to me and we'll see where we get."

"Three weeks ago," the judge said slowly, "five men rode into Pluma. Nobody seems to have seen them— until afterward. But ride in they did. Must have. Rod Stafford, the express messenger, with Karl Peters of the

20

express office, were unloading forty thousand dollars in nice, new, unsigned bills, when these five men swooped down on them in broad daylight—about three in the afternoon it was. There was a short, hot fight. Rod Stafford is a redhead and he would as soon fight nine men as one."

When he stopped and began to fumble in his pocket for a cigar Lace watched shrewdly. He knew men. He felt here an odd undercurrent of emotion. Judge Bettencourt was holding that quiet face, those steady hands, only by a real effort. So he waited for the explanation.

"I know Stafford a little," he said helpfully. "He's no man to take on for a war unless you're dead certain a war's what you really want. What happened to him! He—wasn't killed, was he?"

And he wondered suddenly if Rod Stafford meant anything particular to the judge. Bettencourt had some special interest in this robbery, something more than he had said.

CHAPTER 4

BETTENCOURT SHOOK HIS HEAD. HE DREW IN SMOKE and let it billow out. Lace made a cigarette.

"No. He got a bullet through the neck and a gash in his scalp. But Karl Peters was literally shot to pieces. And the cashier, Winst, was shot through the head. Winst was trying to take a hand in the fight from the back window."

He gestured with the cigar, his pale face very grim. "The particular thing about this gang was its ruthlessness! The five men had scooped up the packages

21

of bills. On their way out of town they saw a man looking through his door at them. They riddled him with bullets—for no reason at all! Then they went out of Pluma like blazes. They simply vanished. The very horses they rode were stolen. The posse discovered them, not twenty miles from town, abandoned. Flying U stock, they were."

"A neat job," Lace conceded, when the judge had stopped. "That is, all but the senseless killing. That kind of puts this gang in a different class. A good little *buscadero*, judge, he tries to get along with no more killing than he has to. But some of the gangs are right cold-blooded; this was one like that."

"You know a great deal about criminals, don't you?"

"Plenty! I ought to. I've ridden on just such jobs as this. No use lying about it. But there was never any killing on any stickup I was in. Happened that way. I've downed two men in my life. But both of them were hard cases that came along picking trouble."

"I told the Governor that you were the one man who knew enough about outlaws—and yet could be trusted—to track down the Pluma robbers! He agreed, if reluctantly. I have here a parole for one Lace Morrow. It will be a full and unconditional pardon, if the Pluma robbers are by the said Morrow delivered—dead or alive—with sufficient proof to convict, to any local or State officer. Does that interest you?"

"Judge!" Lace drawled, leaning forward, "what's up? What's back of this? You're not so dang anxious to see a bunch of bank-robbers and murderers doing the prance, or boarding at the Big House, that it'd make you go chasing to Austin talking the Governor into promising me a pardon. What's the song and dance behind it?"

22

"My nephew, Wes Kincaid, is in Pluma jail, charged with complicity in the robbery," Judge Bettencourt said grimly. "As matters stand at present, he is scheduled to be convicted. That means either a long prison term or— He's not only the wild son of a baby sister, Lace; he's engaged to a girl who is even dearer to me than he is, a girl whom I've always regarded as a daughter."

"What's on him! How come they charged him with the deal?"

"He has been pretty wild. Too wild for a bank teller. Gambling. Losing money. Getting heavily in debt. He was seen talking with some rough customers two days before the robbery. He knew exactly how much money was due and when it would arrive. He and the cashier were the only ones with that knowledge. The only ones in Pluma. Wes took three days' leave against the cashier's wishes. He was very insistent, sulkily so. He said he wanted to go hunting and he was going hunting—and the blazes with the cashier!"

"That all?" Lace asked, for the judge had stopped, as he checked off on his fingers the last points of the evidence.

"Not quite. I said that no usable description was available. But old Elfield, the storekeeper, caught a glimpse of the gang galloping out of town after the robbery. He won't commit himself absolutely, but he saw a rider of Wes Kincaid's general description among the robbers. A man with something white around his neck. And when Wes was arrested, it was within a mile of the abandoned horses and—he had a handkerchief tied around a scratch on his neck."

Lace rolled a cigarette and whistled long and liquidly. He regarded the judge with an ominous head-shaking. "Listen, judge," he said sympathetically. "I can

23

understand how this makes you feel. And I don't know a thing I can say that'll cheer you up—except to hope that the jury trying him is not the same kind that tried me! For they have got plenty to hang him with, if they feel that way. You know that!"

"That's why I went to the Governor when I thought of you. Knowing the outlaws as you do, possibly you could identify those connected with this job. Wes swore to me that he was not in any way, directly or indirectly, connected with the crime. I believe him. I want to believe him, of course. If he is really guilty, your investigation would probably show that. If so, I'll not move so much as a finger to save him. I told the Governor that. He is very bitter about this affair. He and Winst went to college together."

Lace Morrow blew a puff of smoke downward and stared at the toes of his rough shoes. It lured him. The reward—freedom to go and come as he chose in his own state, his own country—was in his eyes tremendous. And he had no sympathy whatever with these grim killers, who had wantonly shot down a gaping townsman.

As he had told the judge, he had in his wild, bitter and reckless youth ridden on raiding expeditions with the *buscaderos*. He had worked for ranchers who paid a bonus of eight or ten dollars for every "slick-ear" brought in by their riders. He had run "wet" cattle and horses over the Mexican line for sale in the States.

But, for all that he had been often on the law's left hand, he could never forget that the Morrows had been tall men in Texas since before the Revolution. He was fundamentally now, at least—a law abiding man. When he had bought the Box M he had asked for nothing but an opportunity to become a peaceable rancher in the

24

Pluma country.

"I'm sorry, judge," he said slowly, after a while. "But I just can't do a thing for you. There are men riding the high lines that I couldn't like a bit better if they were brothers of mine. Men as square as you'd find between this and over where the winds come from. Got pushed into Long Riding same as I was. I can't turn-coat on them, just because I left that life to go straight. Sorry, but—that's flat."

The judge argued desperately. Lace Morrow shrugged heavy shoulders wearily. He felt tired. That pardon, dangling before his inner eye, was a tantalizing thing. But he was stubborn, and he knew that his attitude was the right and decent one. Suddenly, at a certain phrase the judge let drop, Lace straightened and looked sharply at him. He had only half heard what judge Bettencourt said.

"They found a pocketknife," the judge repeated. "A boy saw one of the robbers drop it. It had an odd trademark burned on the stag handle. A sort of C, the lines square-angled. It was worn; the marks were not clear. The sheriff took possession of it."

"Like a square C?" Lace said in a slow thickened voice. He was leaning stiffly now. His red-brown face had gone white and his narrowed eyes were merest slits. The knuckles of his big hands shone pasty-white with the grip he had on his knees. Judge Bettencourt stared at him.

"Yes, like a C a child might make with three straight lines in a boxlike—"

"Box!" Lace interrupted quickly. "That's it! That's the word I was going to use. Like a box, or like half a box. Judge . . . You reckon that sign on the knife could have been that? A half-box? Did you see that knife yourself, or did somebody just tell you about it?"

"Why, I saw it myself," Bettencourt told him, still staring fixedly. "Let's see if I can sketch it exactly, as it was on the knife."

He brought out a memorandum book and pencil from his pocket. Carefully, he outlined a heavy stockknife, then at one end made the rude likeness of the square C he had mentioned. Lace was on his feet, bending over Bettencourt's shoulder the better to stare.

"That was all?" he asked evenly. "Just that?"

"No! Not quite all. It may not have been part of the design, but inside those lines was a smudgy dot. Like this! Now, to be quite honest, that may or may not repesent your half-box. I wouldn't want to convict a man of something that—that obviously you suspect him guilty of, on that evidence. It—"

Lace was grinning now, but it was an utterly humorless grin, almost a cruel lift of hard mouth-corners. He tapped Bettencourt's shoulder imperatively.

"You don't have to convict him. Barto Awe has convicted himself! That Half-Box Dot brand is his mark. That was undoubtedly his mark on the knife. And the senseless killing was like him, too. Judge! I'm giving you a picture of a man changing his mind. You see, Long Riders have got secret signs, and smoke and pictures and telegraph codes. Every man has got his brand. Barto Awe's is what I said—the Half-Box Dot. The reason I wanted to be so sure is this, I sent Barto Awe word two years ago that I would kill him on sight."

He stared blankly and ferociously at the wall beyond the judge. For him it was a picture frame. He could see the happy-go-lucky Bob Vardon, whom Barto Awe had killed from behind for the sake of Bob's share of a poker winning. Lace had hunted his *companero's* killer

26

for a year, but Barto Awe had managed to stay out of sight. Now—

He turned to the judge. "You keep that parole in your pocket. I'll head back to Texas in my own time, my own way. I'll look into this business. Maybe I won't do a thing for you. If I don't, I'll send you word I'm hightailing again. But if Barto Awe turned the trick, I'll bring that crowd in and heave 'em down at your feet and collect my pardon. The State won't be bothered about trying 'em, either. For I'll bring 'em in dead— they pack better that way, anyhow! Barto Awe murdered my best friend."

"But suppose some peace officer, looking for you, picks you up?" the judge frowned, doubtfully. "Don't you think—"

"He'll think he's picked himself a double-handful of cactus," Lace said grimly. "Oh I won't hurt anybody if I can possibly help it. But, you see, judge, I've got to ride the high lines like a man the whole state is hunting. If you want to have me dead, just you let loose one li'l bitsy word about that parole! You can go crawling between the quilts that evening, figuring that I'm lying out somewhere, staring up at the pretty yellow moon— but not seeing it at all."

Judge Bettencourt nodded. "You'll suit yourself, of course. I don't pretend to dictate the course of action that will be best for you."

"No, I'll do that myself," Lace said grimly. "Robbing's the oldest racket in the world. It would be funny if a tolerable system hadn't sprung up, in five-six thousand years. And grapevine telegraphs are all over the country, for all the sheriffs can do. I'll be cutting sticks for Texas, Judge. And once I'm down there, I'll have a look around. I'll try to let you know anything

27

you need to know. And I certainly do hope I'll find that Wes Kincaid is clean on that job."

They shook hands. Then Lace crossed softly to the door and listened for a moment before he opened it. He slipped through, turned to nod, and was gone.

CHAPTER 5

NOBODY IN ANCHO WOULD HAVE RECOGNIZED SAILOR-characteristics in Lace Morrow. He looked exactly what he was—a salty top hand who both would and could mind his own business.

Gone was all the shabby clothing in which he had left San Francisco. A new black Stetson was on the back of his tow head when he rode into the tough little cow-town on the Rio Capitan. New, also, were blue flannel shirt and brown duck pants and tan half-boots. But the twin walnut-handled Colts (one was in a saddle bag, the other cuddled his belly under his shirt) were old and tested companions, like the plain brown saddle and the Winchester carbine forward of his left leg, and Plata, his big gray horse.

He knew Ancho slightly. It was more than sixty miles from Lost Souls Valley where he had been hoping his detective work would make clear the ones responsible for the Pluma bank-robbery and murders. He had never used Ancho much, even in the days when he had been one of the Valley's outstanding visitors, one of Tull Farris' customers in "the Rock House" where Tull sold liquor and staged cowboy-style dances with better-than-you-expected girls for entertainers.

Down the line he had heard of a new county administration in Ancho. The names of the new sheriff

28

and county attorney and county judge meant nothing to him. He felt safe in getting off Plata at the Acme Saloon and crossing the vacant lot on which drowsing horses stood in the late afternoon sunlight.

The Acme was a huge stone-and-adobe building, part-store, part-saloon. A gangling Swede named Anderson, forty years in the country, was proprietor.

Lace went quietly through the door and stopped just inside to look at the handful of men who lined the bar. From a corner of the big, dusky room a high voice rose, that of a Mexican speaking broken English. Looking that way, Lace saw the speaker—a small, dandified, thin-faced man. He sat at a table with a tow-haired cowboy. The two had a deck of cards between them, and money lay on the table before each of them. Apparently they were arguing over whatever game they were playing. The towhead was protesting bitterly, waving his hands. The Mexican reached into his shirt front and produced a short dagger. With a twinkle of shining blade, he drove its point into the table top and it stood there, quivering.

"All right!" the cowboy surrendered. "Have it your own way. But I ain't cutting cards no more with you."

The Mexican jerked his knife loose and returned it to the scabbard under his shirt. He crossed to the end of the bar and halted before a very tall and narrow-shouldered dark man, who had been watching the byplay stonily.

"Lucio Delgado," the Mexican said in his loud rasping voice, "he don't take from any man the arguing. When Lucio Delgado he say he win—! Or somebody he get hurt."

The tall man said nothing. Lace moved down the room, collecting no more than disinterested and

29

mechanical glances from the drinkers. He stopped at the bar almost at that tall, grim and silent man's elbow. Both he and the Mexican looked hard at Lace, Delgado moving around his companion the better to stare. Lace nodded slightly to them.

"Drink?" he asked tonelessly.

The tall man studied him inch by inch with narrow, dull-black eyes, before he nodded. Lucio Delgado said *"Con gusto!"* and went back to his position at the bar's end. Lace signaled the bartender and when a quart and glasses came down to them, he pushed the bottle toward the others. They drank, and Delgado grinned at Lace.

"And now, you will drink one with us."

"Con gusto!" Lace echoed Delgado's own acceptance.

"You speak my tongue?" Delgado cried. "That is very good. For I do not like your damned English!"

Lace said nothing, nor did the tall man speak.

They had several drinks and Delgado rattled on, sometimes in Spanish to Lace, again in broken English to his companion, whom he called "Topeka." And at last, without a word, Topeka left them, going with long, unhurried steps toward the opening into the store. Delgado grinned and jerked a thumb at the other's narrow back.

"He is a very quiet man, that Topeka Gates. I have never ridden with him for three days before. And never will I ride so long with him again! He tires me. *Amor de dios*, how he tires me. I talk, and he looks. I talk, and he looks again. Never a word! He is one to think always of the business. That, I think is why he was chosen—"

He stopped short and his full-lidded eyes came suspiciously sidelong to Lace's inscrutable face. Lace

30

shrugged.

"I am like you. I do not care to ride with a man who cannot pass the time of day pleasantly. Do you know this country? The several towns and—the important men?"

But Lucio Delgado had evidently decided that for once he had talked too much. He shook his head. He was a stranger, too, he said in regretful tone. Topeka Gates, also, was a stranger.

Lace nodded as if it made no difference. But he had ridden the high lines far too long not to recognize the signs of men who rode on some private business. And, judging the two—so much alike of thin, cruel mouths— he automatically dismissed the thought that the oddly-assorted pair might be officers on someone's trail. He considered Ancho . . .

"Nothing much here to draw a *buscadero*," he decided. "The bank, of course. But it would be hard to crack, sitting there in the middle of town with the sheriff's office right next to it. And old Anderson, here, has got a regular fort when he puts up the shutters and locks his doors. I—wonder."

Delgado went out to the street. Lace loafed upon the bar for a while. The bartender, evidently, had noted his talk with Delgado. He came down, polishing a glass. He looked into the store, then leaned slightly to Lace. He spoke huskily, "I take it you do'no' that Mexican. He's getting to be a plumb nuisance and the Old Man had ought to give him the bum's rush before we get us a killing in here. Him and that big feller he calls Topeka, this is the second day they been in here. Delgado is always starting a row with folks that ain't bothering him. Thought I'd tell you the kind he is."

"Thanks," Lace said in a grateful tone. "They act like

31

a couple officers looking for somebody. Only the Mexican's not the kind I'd pick for a deputy if I happened to be a sheriff. Which—" he added with a grin—"lord knows I never was and never want to be."

"Feller come in yesterday," the bartender told him without much interest. "Says they're looking for a man named Dave Crews. They was asking down at the livery corral if Crews had come to town lately. Liveryman told 'em he hadn't seen Crews in six months. Told 'em Crews has got a one-cow ranch over on Animas Creek above Lost Souls Valley."

"Wonder they wouldn't go over there then," Lace drawled, keeping his own tone as disinterested as the bartender's.

A drinker came in, drawing the bartender away. Lace stared at his own reflection in the mirror. Dave Crews . . . He knew very well the gangling Dave Crews, agent of Tull Farris, who was boss of Lost Souls Valley. The little ranch on the Animas was a regular stopping-place for Long Riders. Crews furnished Farris information from which Farris could scheme robberies at points far distant from the Valley hang-out.

So, if Topeka Gates and Lucio Delgado were waiting in Ancho for Crews, they were *buscaderos*, doubtless from Lost Souls Valley. Since some gang or other—or several at once used the cabins in Farris' hide-out for twelve months of the year, Delgado and Gates might even be members of Barto Awe's gang. That thought made Lace's pulses jump.

Now a man got up from where, apparently, he had been sleeping across chairs against the thick wall opposite the bar. He was red of face and hair, hazel-eyed, fat. He wore new overalls, loose-fitting, that made his width seem enormous. For the rest of him there was nothing to note. He put on a shabby gray hat and waddled across to the bar. His eyes roved to Lace. He grinned disarmingly.

"Have one?" he invited Lace, with a jerk of his head toward the bar. "Hate to drink by myself."

His name was Curly Camp and he was from Idaho. But originally he had been a Montana man. He talked ramblingly of the northern ranges. Lace claimed Arizona for his native range—and wondered if Camp were lying as smoothly. But there was nothing about the fat man's round, innocent face to make him seem anything but the puncher he said he was.

He was not giving all his attention to Camp, anyway. He thought of Gates and Delgado—and of Dave Crews. He wondered why he had not remembered Crews before this. The lanky rancher was a store-house of *buscadero* information. He would know exactly who was in the Valley at the Rock House; he would have heard—at least he would have satisfied his mind—about the men responsible for the Pluma robbery. The only difficulty would be in getting him to talk.

Lace wondered if it would be a good policy to make himself known as one of the fraternity to Delgado and Gates. That was a simple matter. As he had told Judge Bettencourt in San Francisco, the riders of the high lines had their own means of recognizing one another.

He decided to keep away from the two for the time being. Better to watch for Crews and try to talk privately to the nester. He nodded to Camp. "See you some more. Want to put my horse in the corral. He ought to be ready for the supper bell about now."

He went out and around to where Plata stood under the cottonwood. When he had mounted and come back to the street, he looked toward the Acme's door. Curly

Camp stood there. The fat man waved and Lace nodded to him.

There was nobody but a crippled hostler in sight, in the dusty yard of the livery corral. He showed Lace a stall for the gray and got feed for him. When he had hobbled away, leaving Lace beside Plata in the stall, Lace began to prowl about the corral. He found two horses which—from the length of the leathers on the saddles hanging beside them he guessed were the mounts of Delgado and Gates. He listened at the entrance of that stall and, hearing nothing, quietly investigated the saddle bags on both saddles. There was nothing but soiled or extra clothing in either, with tobacco and shells for .44 and .45 guns, until—he held up the length of narrow manila paper and grinned. "Enough to hang you, Topeka!" he said softly. For it was in the tall man's *alforja* that his probing fingers had discovered that money wrapper from the Langston City Bank, with its legend printed in blue letters. "Yes, sir! Enough to hang you."

He went out of the stall and moved softly about the place, but found no trace of the two he hunted. So he went back to the Acme and had a drink with Camp, who was leaning on the bar discussing saloons with the bartender.

Neither Delgado nor Gates came in. Lace and Camp went to supper at a Chinese eating house when it was dark. Camp mentioned the tall man and his noisy companion. Lace shrugged.

"I've rambled too much," he said, "to figure that a Mexican may not be just as good a man as you'd want to side. This Delgado may be as hard a case as he thinks he is."

CHAPTER 6

ANCHO, TO THE DRIFTING COWBOY, SEEMED TO OFFER little in the way of amusement except what could be found in the saloons. There was not even a dance-hall running, so Camp informed Lace at the table. One was supposed to open up within a week or so, but for the present a little gambling and the usual drinking were all that could be expected.

"Then let's see what kind of poker players we can scare up," Lace said resignedly. "Wonder if Pluma is better than Ancho? You come through there?"

"Yeh. It's some livelier but not what I'd call a hurrah town at that. Poker'll suit me fine, if it ain't too stiff."

They found Delgado and the tall, silent Topeka Gates at the Acme's bar. Delgado seemed to be half-drunk. He was talking to a dull-faced young man who wore a sheriff's star on a spotted cowhide vest. Topeka merely stood in his usual moveless, uninterested fashion beside the two.

Lace asked them if poker appealed and the sheriff nodded. He had been drinking, too. It was apparent in his thick tone. Delgado grinned wolfishly.

"I will be glad to gamble with you, *hombre*," he told Lace. "But before we begin I will warn you both that I am very good at poker and that I am not a man to argue. *Por dios*! I could tell of a time—or a dozen times—in Mexico when I needed to show what manner of man I am at gambling. Do not sit with me at poker, if your stomachs are not strong, or if you do not like to lose. And lose without argument . . . ."

"Ah, I reckon we'll take a chance," Curly Camp said with wide and cheerful grin. "You likely are worse on the bark than the bite."

"Didn't know you slung the Spanish," Lace told him with a curious side-glance. "Not so many Mexicans on the northern ranges, I thought."

"I make out. Worked on the Tongue-Block with a half dozen Mexicans. Picked up the *chili* lingo easy. You playing, fella?"

Topeka shook his head. Dull eyes came to Delgado. Lace saw without seeming to look. Topeka seemed to be reminding Delgado of something with that glance.

"Not to let his tongue rattle so much, probably," Lace decided. "Well, with both of'em in sight, Dave Crews oughtn't to get away from me if he comes to town."

They sat down with a greasy deck of cards, Lace, Curly, the sheriff, Delgado and two cowboys from the Spur outfit. The game was stud and Delgado proved himself what he had claimed to be, a good player. For a while Lace had no cards. Then Delgado cleaned one of the Spur men—a small straight against three aces. The cowboy got up, shaking his head.

"Them aces," he said ruefully, "they looked bigger'n that many mountains. But that was then! Count me out gents."

Delgado shifted into the vacated chair. He had his back to the thick wall separating saloon from store. He faced the bar, while Lace had his back to it—and to Topeka. The sheriff ordered a quart of whisky and glasses for them all.

"No use being a sheriff," he told them boozily, "if you can't make money at it. And no use making money if you don't spend it. Everybody in Ancho County knows me. They know I'll wear out the edges on my dollars, rolling'em."

Topeka, Lace saw by shifting occasionally in his

36

chair, was also drinking—steadily. Curly looked up at the tall man, then across at Delgado. He grinned. "Never would've believed it!" he said. "Your big side-kick is talking! Yes, sir, really talking!"

"Bravo Trail!" Topeka was saying in a thick, slow voice to the bartender. "*Camino del bravo*, they call it in Sonora. Took a good man to ride it. I met a fella—"

His voice droned on while the stud deal shifted from man to man at the table. Lace heard him without thinking about him. He heard him describe the argument he had with the man met on that *camino del bravo*.

"Had my gun under my leg," Topeka informed bartender and drinkers. "Watched him. And when he couldn't see I was heeled, he went for his and—"

There was the roar of a pistol at the bar. Lace flung himself sideways, as did Lucio Delgado. Both sprawled upon the floor. Topeka stood with smoking Colt in his hand, staring at them. The sheriff, who had been on Lace's left, twisted his face and groped under the table.

"Dang' slug burned my leg," he said in a surprised voice. "Who was doing that shooting, anyhow?"

"Thumb must've slipped!" Topeka told them generally. His tone held more of surprise than the sheriff's. "Funny! Never did know that to happen before. Dang' funny!"

"Put it away!" the sheriff commanded. "Good thing you're a friend of Delgado's. Put you in the *juz gado*, if you wasn't. You're drunk. I don't like a man can't handle his liquor. Put it away and go set down somewhere. Make us nervous, playing with that cutter like that!"

Topeka nodded meekly. He replaced the gun in its spring holster under his arm. The sheriff waved him to a chair in a corner and Topeka slouched that way. Curly shook his head, staring after the tall figure with his habitual grin.

"Wouldn't want to sleep with that fella when he'd really took hisself a load," he said. "He'd fight San Jacinto all over again and likely shoot a man into strips."

Lace looked with blank face at Topeka. He was pretty certain of two things, when he had studied the man's walk. Topeka was not drunk. And that shot had been no accident. Its course had been past his hip and so across the sheriff's leg.

He looked across at Lucio Delgado and met a calculating stare in the Mexican's dark eyes. But Delgado grinned and pushed the cards over.

"It is your deal. And—if you do not mind, keep your hands higher while you deal. Last time, they were very close to the edge of the table. It does not look well, that."

"Sorry," Lace apologized. "Just an accident."

"Oh, I will tell any man—once, when I do not like his manner of dealing," Delgado said smilingly. "Once . . .

Both he and Lace had kings when the deal was halted. Delgado pushed in a gold piece. Lace and Curly saw the bet. Lace dropped an ace on Delgado's cards, a nine of spades on Curley's, a king on his own. He pushed in fifty dollars. Curly withdrew, groaning. Delgado fumbled with a belt under his shirt and got out a handful of twenties. He spilled them in the tables center and grinned at Lace. "And one hundred dollars more!"

"It cleans me to see that," Lace told him, grinning. "If I had it, I'd raise you. I—"

"You would be foolish. For you have but the pair of kings and a hole-card which is the deuce of clubs or spades. I saw it fall. And I have the pair of kings with an

38

ace!"

He put out his right hand to the money and began to draw it toward him. Lace shook his head. "Your eyes are not so good. I have another king in the hole, not a deuce. And so—"

"I *said* that I tell a man once, when I do riot like his dealing. And so—"

His elbow jerked—his left elbow. Lace had watched him from the moment that he had seen Topeka sit down in the corner. That "accidental" shot had been intended for him. He was certain of it. So his own right hand had been on the table edge very close to the open front of his shirt.

Now, that hand went with a speed none in Ancho was likely to match, inside the shirt, to grip the butt of the pistol in his waistband. But interruption came, before either man's gun jumped above the table. Curly, sitting on Delgado's left, twisted in his chair. His left hand flashed out of sight beneath the table and his right hand—closed into a big fist—hooked up to Delgado's jaw. A pistol bellowed beneath the table, but Delgado went over sideways, falling across the sheriff, and carrying the officer with him to the floor. The sheriff scrambled up, but Delgado sprawled limp and motionless. Curly turned his round face upon Lace.

"The son of a dog had his pistol out, a-lying on his lap, before he ever put that money in the pot," he said almost apologetically.

"Thanks," Lace grunted. He was looking toward that corner where Topeka had sat down, but there was no sign of the tall roan now.

He stood then, pushing back his chair. He moved past the sheriff, who swayed on his feet and blinked vacantly from one to the other of them. Over his shoulder, Lace spoke briefly to Curly. "Pick up that money for me, will you? I want to see just what this little sidewinder's really packing."

He bent over Delgado after he had scooped up the pistol which had dropped from the Mexican's hand. Another, shorter, Colt was in Delgado's waistband, under the shirt, in back. And he had the wicked dagger which Lace had seen him draw to intimidate that tow-haired cowboy.

"I reckon you'd better take care of these, Sheriff," Lace said to that worthy.

Then he stooped again, to catch Delgado by one wrist and one ankle. He carried him up the bar-room and, stopping in the open door, swung him back and forth for an instant, then threw him clear across the sidewalk, to land in the dust of the street. He was turning back when, from somewhere in the darkness around the back door, there was a shot.

Lace went to the floor—flashingly, automatically. He heard that bullet whine past his face, and down the clear center of the bar-room he fired twice at the door.

There was no second shot from the darkness. Without speaking to anyone, Lace went quickly down to listen at that door, which gave upon an unlit store-room—or so the bartender informed him eagerly, without being asked.

"Seems to me," the bartender added, "I heard a horse running out there, after that shot. I wouldn't swear to it, but it does seem to me I heard someone riding off."

"I wouldn't be a bit surprised if you're right," Lace told him dryly. "Well, Sheriff? Anything you think about?"

"Couldn't hold his liquor," the sheriff said abruptly. "The blazes with a man that can't hold his liquor, I say!

That long-coupled jigger and Delgado both. I thought
Delgado was all right. But he couldn't hold his liquor,
neither. The blazes with both of'em. You're all right!"

And with that he lurched to the bar and clawed at a
quart standing there.

Lace looked steadily at Curly. Then he made a slight
head motion and went toward the front door. The fat
cowboy trailed him. They stood just outside the door for
an instant. Curly leaned a little toward Lace.

"The Mexican," he whispered, "has also gone from
our midst. Likely, Gates and Delgado had their horses
saddled and standing out back when we come into the
place."

"I wouldn't bet a nickel that you could be wrong,"
Lace assured him grimly. "Thanks for putting him on
the floor. But—*he* owes you something, too."

"Yeh. That's right," Curly admitted. "But I acted kind
of on the point of the minute, you might say. I just
happened to look down, and see him with that gun on
his lap. I couldn't be sure you had seen it. If you hadn't,
he had all the edge on you, and that didn't set right with
me. But when you made that out-of-the-waistband
draw—Yeah, I saved his life, all right."

"Thanks just the same," Lace told him, and grinned.
"Now, I think they both hit the trail. They've been
waiting here two days to see a man—Oh, you knew
about that, too!"

For Curly laughed softly.

CHAPTER 7

"I WAS KIND OF WONDERING ABOUT 'EM, YOU SEE," Curly explained amusedly. "So I asked a question—or maybe six—and kind of added up what answers I got. Then I made the usual cut in case I happened to get to talking to a liar. But the answer was still a high-pocketed nester, name of Dave Crews. They expected to meet Crews here. Why, I do'no'. Maybe you do?"

Lace whistled softly and stared at this fat man who was developing characteristics not indicated either by his heavy body or by his round guileless face.

"You know, I'm sort of wondering about you—wondering if you're exactly what you look to be."

Curly laughed again, and shrugged heavy shoulders. "We used to have an old preacher back home that always said nothing was like it looked to be . . . So, likely I'm not what you might take me for. And—I wouldn't be a bit surprised if that same would go for you . . . But, I do tell you this. If, for some reason or other you're interested in the men that're interested in this Dave Crews, and if there's any little thing I could do—I haven't got a place in the world I got to go, and no time at all that I've got to get there. I like your style fine. So, if you want somebody to side you—?"

"You don't know how much I'd like to have somebody I could trust, riding along with me where I'm headed. Somebody about your size and shape and all, siding me! But—no, I can't take you up, Curly. Wouldn't be fair. What I am—where I have to go—what I have got to do—no. But I do thank you and I certainly would like to have you along, any other time.

Now—"

"Maybe this might change your notions some," Curly told him softly.

His forefinger made a jerky motion against his blue jumper front. Lace stared. Again Curly made that outline and Lace said in a slow, incredulous tone, "But I thought you stayed north. In fact, I thought they snared you in Montana."

"Five years in Deer Lodge," Curly agreed. "But when I had done three of it, the Governor offered me a pardon if I'd promise never to hit a lick inside his state again. And the reason I headed south was not because I was hunting a climate to fit my clothes, exactly. They elected an old boy sheriff in my home county in Wyoming and I used to bust broncs with him, and he saved me from being drug to death one time. I just didn't feel like cracking down in his bailiwick. And so—I thought I'd take a look at Lost Souls Valley. Tie in with a good bunch, or get three-four good boys together and cash in on my six-shooter."

"We heard a lot about you when I was riding with the Smoky Hills Gang," Lace said marvelingly. "That Streaky Lightning sign of yours will take you a long way, even down here on the Bravo Trail. Curly Cole . . . Camp's just your go-by, I take it? I never heard of it being used by you."

"No, Cole was the go-by. Camp's my real name. So you forked it with the Smoky Hills outfit . . . I don't make you—"

"Lace Morrow. I never put my sign as far north as your part of the world. You could take it for a hat, but it's supposed to be the sun halfway up above the line."

"I know you," Curly assured him. "Well? Now that we're this far along, what's next? What's all this you

43

want to do?"

"The first thing is to locate this long-coupled nester Dave Crews that Delgado and Gates are waiting for. I want to chew the rag with Dave and see what I can find out about who is using the Valley right now. If you want to trail along—"

When Curly nodded, they stepped off the sidewalk and Curly got his horse, a thick-barreled gelding of bay so dark as to seem black in the dusk.

"He'll pack double. Climb up behind as far as the corral," Curly invited Lace.

They jogged downstreet to the livery corral and Lace paid the crippled hostler. This one looked curiously at him.

"Them men that went out awhile ago, they was kind of auguring about you," he told Lace. "Seems like they seen you looking at their hulls in the stall. They never liked it."

"That fancy big horn kak with all the silver would make anybody take a second look," Lace said in a surprised voice. "What did they say about me?"

"The Mexican was going right out to take a looky and cut your heart out. But the other man pulled him off and done a lot of talking I couldn't hear. The Mexican laughed and they went out. I kind of figured they maybe had got to you, when they left town so fast a little bit back."

"Did Dave Crews come in?" Lace asked, on impulse.

"No. Dave ain't been in Ancho since Heck was a spotted pup. But they did say something about him being surely due tonight. And they rode right past awhile ago, heading toward Pluma. Maybe they'll meet him on the road."

Lace thanked him and mounted Plata. He and Curly

took the road indicated by the hostler and rode through the darkness.

"I'm not a curious hairpin," Curly said after a while. "If there's something special about all this that you don't want to talk about—?"

"It's pretty special," Lace admitted. "But I don't mind telling you what's what. You said you know me. But I take it you don't know a lot; about as much as that I rode with that Smoky Hills outfit and all?"

"Just about that. Fellas'd drift into my country with a tale about the *buscaderos* down here. You know how the talk runs: this fella's a born killer and even his sidekicks had better watch him, that one's a good man and he went on the dodge because of this or that or something else—That's the way I heard about you, now and then. And what I heard made me willing to throw in with you—even more willing than I was from sizing you up in the saloon."

"When I was a kid," Lance told him slowly, staring straight ahead and almost unseeingly, "my father and I lived on a little ranch close to Pluma. He got killed and the mortgage wasn't in good shape. So the bank took over the place and I started saddle-tramping. You know how that is for a fourteen-year old kid. Either makes or breaks him. It made a Hand out of me. Well, I made some friends that were riding the high lines. Good men, good friends. I did'em favors sometimes, warned'em when the John Laws were around, packed grub to'em. And when I was eighteen I killed me a tough deputy sheriff that was trying to get a rep by collecting safe tail feathers. I went on the dodge. Had to! They would've hung me in that part of Arizona . . ."

Curly grunted understanding.

"Well, the Smoky Hills outfit was the bunch of

45

friends I mentioned. I began to ride with Smoky and the others. But nobody ever could *prove* a thing on me. Then while I was separated from 'em, they got wiped out. Most of 'em. All the regulars. I thought it over and decided that I was safe from that Arizona murder charge, the witnesses and all being dead or scattered. I came back home to Pluma and bought a one-cow ranch. The bank was stuck up in Darien and the private detectives had to do something. So they claimed I had a part in it, staked the job for the actual robbers. I got twenty years—"

He told Curly of his escape from Sheriff Roy Jacks, of his wanderings, of meeting first Jacks, then Judge Bettencourt, in San Francisco, of the offer he had accepted.

"That was a hard thing," Curly said drawlingly. "But in your shoes I would have done the same thing, said the same thing. It's not like turning Law and using all you have got from men that trusted you, to hang 'em or send 'em up. You are just getting what the Mex' call a *pelon*, an extra, for doing what you'd do anyhow. And I'm like you. I don't hold with killing. I know a lot about Barto Awe and the kind of killers that he picks to side him."

He laughed grimly. "I know a lot about him. I knew plenty five years back, when this country got too hot for him and he decided he'd try the northern range a spell. I sent him a word to stay out unless he wanted to fight me as well as the Johns. And he must've heard something about me. For he turned back. I wasn't going to have him raising hell up there. Well! I'm with you. I'll help all I can at the detective work. This Dave Crews, now. You've got a reason for meeting him?"

Lace explained Crews' part in the Valley's life, and his own old acquaintance with the nester. "He ought to know everything I need to know. Question is will he tell me? He ought not to worry about talking to me. I'm an old-timer in Lost Souls Valley. Besides everybody knows that I'm facing twenty years and only beat it by the runout I took on Roy Jacks. But he's a funny son, Dave is. Risk his neck getting whatever it is Tull Farris wants to know. But yellow in most other ways. Scared to death of Tull Farris and the kind that work with Tull. But he'll stand up, scared stiff, and argue that his cut of the job ought to be bigger than it is."

"Was that a shot?" Curly asked suddenly. "Sounded like it to me! A long way ahead . . ."

"Maybe Delgado and Gates bumped into trouble before they bumped into Dave Crews," Lace said cheerfully." "I could stand their funerals without even straining a hamstring!"

But it was not the two they followed, sprawling in the road. A riderless horse grazing beside the trail stiffened Lace and Curly. They went on quietly, cautiously, to where a man lay in the dust. While Curly stood guard, watching the darkness all around, Lace got down to strike a match and hold the flame cupped in his hand near the fallen one's face.

"This," he said slowly, as much to himself as to Curly, "sort of changes things around. This is Dave Crews. Delgado and Gates wanted to see him to kill him. They met him and—"

Search of the dead man produced nothing. A leather money belt which Lace had often seen about his waist was missing, and the shirt jerked from his cheap cotton pants seemed to tell of its removal after his death. He had been shot through the head.

"Let's lash him on that horse of his," Lace suggested. "I don't want him found here, on the road we took out of Ancho. We might be blamed for it just as soon as Delgado and Gates."

When they had quirted the horse off with its swaying rider, Curly grunted inquiringly.

"I'm going into the Valley," Lace told him decisively. "This lick at Crews is some of Tull Farris' work. Maybe Delgado and Gates are back there now. Maybe not. But that's the only place I can hope to find out anything about Barto Awe, or the killings and robbery."

"You mean—*we'll* go into the Valley," Curly corrected him.

"Of course. But not together. I'll go one way and get in ahead of you. Then you'll drift in. We'll both be *buscaderos*, and entitled to come in. But we won't look like a partnership. There's a straight trail in—if you know it—from a place not five miles from here. Then there's a longer trail that I'll tell you about. That'll be yours. And when you come in, you'll find me already there. We'll look at each other and laugh."

"Because we run into one another at Ancho, but didn't trust what we saw," Curly checked him, nodding. "A good idea. For if Delgado and Gates are back in the Valley, with this Tull Farris, they'll probably tell him about the little deal in Ancho, when they tried to rub out your mark and couldn't quite get there. All right. Give me the trail."

They rode on until Lace found his landmark, a pile of whitish boulders. Beyond these a very web of stock-trails wound through the greasewood. Lace sent Plata up one taken at random and Curly followed.

"There's your road," Lace said presently. "I go straight ahead. I'll expect you some time day after tomorrow. *Adios*!"

"Be seeing you," Curly called back. "Watch your neck!"

48

CHAPTER 8

WHEN A WINCHESTER WHANGED ABOVE HIM, AND A bullet skipped across the trail before Plata, Lace pulled in the big gray calmly. He stared sidewise up the slope toward the sheltered top of Lookout Rock. Again the long gun sounded and a slug splatted upon a nearby rock. Lace raised his right hand high, palm toward the Rock.

This was merely the regular precaution. He had expected some outlaw sentry to challenge him from the lookout. It would be a dull half-year that Tull Farris did not play "host" to some Long Rider outfit, in the Rock House known from Wyoming to the Rio Grande as a hide-out safe from the most bulldogged sheriff or marshal. Hard-eyed men, quick-triggered; men who rode the "high lines" when they moved—Lookout Rock and Lost Souls Valley were known to all of them.

Lace waited for the other formalities.

A .45-90 barrel came sliding like a brown snake from a clump of brush twenty feet uphill from Lace. Half-absently, Lace was singing that lament of outland men known from the Selkirks away to the Old Trail of Southern Mexico.

The hands of the sentry were copper-colored. A thick forefinger cuddled the trigger of the rifle. Lace's eyes narrowed—you might think that hairpin was about to let go.

"Who you?" a guttural voice demanded—a truculent kind of voice. It assured Lace that he was dealing now with an Indian.

"Lace Morrow!" he grunted. He did not fancy those Indians he had seen among the Long Rider outfits—

Osages, Comanches, Cherokees, or mixtures. Too savage, too uncertain. "Don't get so nervous with that trigger, you! Who's in Little Cabin?"

"Dang' tough bunch! From Utah. Why I no down you, huh?"

"Listen," Lace said more grimly still. "Where the blazes are you from? You trying to tell me you never heard of me? Never heard of the Smoky Hills outfit? Who's in this tough bunch of yours, anyway?"

"No hear of Lace Morrow! Don' give a dang! No hear of Smoky Hills gang. Don' give a dang! Me Frio. Bad man. Better I kill you now!"

Lace knew that he was actually on the ragged edge of death. This sullen, bloodthirsty Indian believed that a dead man was a safe man. Evidently he was sentry for some hard case outfit holed up in Little Cabin, some bunch to whom Lace Morrow was unknown. Strangers, to this fellow, were all potential spies.

"Who's that?" Lace demanded suddenly.

"Hah?" Frio's head jerked about. As the rifle muzzle wavered, out came the Colts from Lace's holsters. The pistols roared—right hand, left hand. Frio howled.

He had a twice-hit gunhand and, with a surge, Plata went forward. Lace bent from the saddle and cracked the Indian over the head with a Colt barrel. For an instant he looked dourly down, then shifted in the saddle.

"A tough bunch?" he said between his teeth. "*Por dios*, I'll have something to say about their putting a fool Indian on watch!"

He rode on up the trail to its crest and where it turned to dip into the lovely, hidden valley, he drew rein. "Come on out," he said quietly. "There's just one of me. I left your watchdog back yonder—and a hell of a sentry

50

he turned out to be—no sense, no salt, nothing!"

"Who the blazes you think you are, popping your mouth off so free?" a squat, black man snarled, coining out from behind a boulder with Winchester half-raised. "Frio's my man—"

"You'd be saying *was*, if I didn't happen to be soft-hearted," Lace replied. "Most men would've killed him."

The squat leader of the Utah men had the advantage. Lace watched with a small, contemptuous smile, thumbs hooked in his cartridge belt. He had to draw to get into action. But the dark man waived the advantage of his pointing Winchester.

"My name's Morrow, Lace Morrow. Your Frio says he never heard of me. The rest of you all green in this country, too?"

"We're from the Green River country. Over there they call me 'Tulsa Jack.' Things got too cluttered up with U. S. Marshals and their likes. So we lit a shuck this way. We knowed about the Little Cabin, of course, from other riders. About Lost Souls Valley and Tull Farris."

"Well, if you all play the damn' fool like you been doing here, acting like you own the place," Lace said scornfully, "you'll last in the valley about as long as the tissue paper pup that chased the cast iron cat through hell. We've got our ways down here. Outsiders fit into those ways nice and polite—or else—"

"Say! You waggle that slit under your nose a lot!" a new voice remarked angrily. "You—"

"Come out from behind that rock if you want to wawa with me!" Lace invited him. "Come out and let's see how high you stand and what you weigh, dressed!"

"Hold your horses, Noisy," the squat leader snapped,

as a huge, red-faced man bounded into the open. "I never hear of this hairpin before, but he acts like one of our kind. What's your road sign, Morrow?"

"Like this," Lace told him, and with forefinger outlined it upon his shirt. "You can call it a half-circle on a bar. It's the sun halfway up above the rim."

"I remember it," Tulsa Jack said with a frown of concentration. "Saw it once on Castle Rock."

"Well, let's go on down to the cabin. I've been away a while—quite a while. But I've slept more nights in the Little Cabin than in lots of rooming houses I know. Oh! Better tell that nitwit, Frio, that even if he never heard of Lace Morrow, plenty around here have. Tell him not to start painting up for war unless he's dead certain war's the thing he can't do without!"

Noisy made a snarling sound and said nothing.

"You tell him that, Noisy!" Tulsa Jack commanded. "No rowing in the Valley with men that belong in the Valley. Go on up to the Rock and take the guard. Send Frio down to me."

"How many men with you?" Lace asked carelessly. But he was interested in knowing if Delgado and Gates belonged to this Utah gang.

"There's five of us altogether. Frio and Noisy you know about. Dynamite's cooking down at the cabin. Then I got a kid name' Lanny. He's moving the horses, now. We got in yesterday. Been resting up. Aim to head down into the Valley tomorrow. I sent Lanny down with word to Tull Farris. Farris said to come on down."

"Who was on guard here when you rode up?" Lace asked curiously. "One of the old-timers?"

"Name was Tom Elton," Tulsa said with a shrug. "Do'no' if he was old in the Valley or not. He never said. Li'l black fella and he never seemed much on the talk."

"He's not," Lace agreed dryly. "Never was much on the talk, Tom Elton wasn't. But he's plain murder on the fight. As good a man as I would ask for, to side me in a tight. He's as old around here as I am."

Then in a casual voice he asked, "How'd you fellows come up? Straight over from Green River, or did you stop to do a job or so on the way?"

It was as if a mask had dropped over Tulsa's dark, square face. His murky eyes were as steady, as blank, as a snake's. And there ws no tone to his voice when he said, "Oh, we come straight over. But, of course, when I say straight, I don't mean we just rode day and night. There was a lot of time that we did our serious riding after it got good and dark. You know how that is."

There was no more expression on Lace's face than upon Tulsa's, as he nodded with that evasive answer. Tulsa had no intention of discussing his gang's activities with a stranger. That was very clear.

Ever since passing the fringes of this lawless section, he had moved as a detective on the trail. Long before making Ancho he had begun to sound out those who might know of Long Riders' "jobs," inquiring diplomatically about various robberies, and the men concerned in them. But he had received not a word of really definite information concerning the Pluma robbery. Either the nesters and the occasional *buscaderos* encountered on the trail knew nothing about the background of that job, or else Lace Morrow was considered a man apart because of his two years of honesty.

Not that he had been able to find any real difference in old acquaintances' treatment of him. Everyone in this country seemed to remember him as the Lace Morrow

53

of amazing speed and skill at gunplay, the roan who had ridden with the swaggering, hard case outfit of Smoky Hills and, finally, as that convicted bank-robber who had made a fool of the famous sheriff, bulldogged Roy Jacks.

Because of all this, well before riding into Ancho he had begun to wonder if that Pluma job had not been the work of some outside gang, strangers to the Pluma-Ancho neighborhood. And, he told himself now, if it had been an outside gang, why not this tough outfit of Tulsa Jack's? It seemed to him that the murderous Frio, the red-haired Noisy, even this squat, dark man beside him, were quite capable of such a robbery as that, including the useless and cold-blooded killing of that curious citizen who had merely looked out of his door.

But, if they did pull the Pluma job, then hightailed it here to the Valley to hole up, Tulsa's not going to admit it. If it was this gang behind that job—instead of Barto Awe's—the chances are Tull Farris will know about it.

Thought of the Valley's boss opened up a whole new avenue of speculation. Tull Farris kept an eye on the movements of all Long Riders who chanced to be in his neighborhood. If newcomers made a profitable haul, they either paid for shelter in the Valley of Lost Souls or—they met with trouble . . . And Tulsa had said that Tull Farris had sent him word to come on into the Valley.

That meant one of two things: either Tulsa's gang rode with heavy pockets from the Pluma bank, and had agreed to make a split with the boss of the Valley, or they had done no job in this neighborhood and were being received merely as strangers who might fit into some of Farris' schemes.

Either way, there was no answer to these questions to

54

be found, except down in the Valley at Farris' Rock House. Unless, of course, he could surprise Tulsa or some other Green River man into making a slip.

"Yeh, Tull Farris told us to come on down. He said he's got something real big on," Tulsa said as they moved along the trail. "The way he talked to Lanny, he must have a right fat hen on. There's other Long Riders in the Valley, I hear. But Farris thinks this job has got plenty in it for everybody. And—the more, the safer."

"Depends on who makes up the crowd," he said without showing particular interest. "Often, three or four good men can handle a job that a dozen not-so-goods will fumble."

He saw the angry side-glance that Tulsa turned on him and, inwardly, he grinned. It was part of his pose to take this hard case attitude with everyone he met. Particularly, he had to be "on the prod" in the Valley. Belligerence with such an outfit as Tulsa Jack's was his very best weapon. And that would be true in dealing with the other Long Riders he expected to find in Tull Farris' Rock House.

CHAPTER 9

SO AS THEY WENT ON TOWARD LITTLE CABIN, HE WAS amused at the proof of his power to irritate the Utah man. If he could keep Tulsa and Noisy and the others angry because of his swaggering manner they would be less likely to suspect him of playing the detective.

"Naturally," he told Tulsa with something like good-humored contempt, "any man who rode as one of Smoky Hills' regulars has a different way of looking at things. When it comes to grading the Long Riders, old

Smoky stood way up at the head of the class. And nobody but the best men could ride with him."

Tulsa let that pass. For it was true. Any "regular" of Smoky Hills was a tall man in Long Rider company. He was quiet for a while. Then he grinned at Lace.

"Don't worry about Noisy none," he said. "He's pretty loose-holstered and all, and when he don't like a man he goes right on the fight. But when he gets to know you—"

Lace laughed, facing Tulsa squarely. "If he's any use to you, my advice is to pass that word along to him. Don't bother about me! Nothing that comes out of Utah is likely to worry Lace Morrow—or anybody else out of the Long Riders in this neck of the woods. Not one li'l bitsy worry!"

Tulsa Jack scowled malignantly under Lace's contemptuous tone. Lace, observing the clawing of the dark man's pistol hand, made a tiny left-handed gesture.

"The sky's the limit, any time you want to pop your whip," he said calmly. "I say anything I feel like saying —and oftentimes I feel like saying a whole lot. But there's one thing I do hang to—the sky's your limit any time you don't like something I say. You can go the limit."

For a long minute Tulsa continued to stare savagely at Lace. Then, as if moved by some private thought, he grinned.It was not a pleasant lip-stretching, nor was the light in his murky eyes good-humored.

"Yeh, that's right," he said. "I certainly can. And you—you can hope that nothing ever comes out of the Green River country, or anywhere else, to worry you." And for the rest of the way to Little Cabin, he whistled quite cheerfully to himself.

Swinging down before the familiar door of the log

house on its knoll, Lace looked around curiously. Nothing had changed since his last days here with Smoky Hills. But he had gone south from the cabin; Smoky Hills had ridden into the north like some scarred and suspicious old *lobo*. There had been death waiting for the grizzled outlaw in just such another cabin up on the Canadian. But the two—the old Long Rider and the young—had parted with no particular thought of that. Lace turned abruptly with Tulsa's repeated word.

"Yeah," he answered slowly, "like I said, I've slept here many's the time."

Old Smoky Hills had preached what amounted to a full sermon on outlawry, that day before they went their separate ways. He had advised Lace to leave the high lines before be was so branded that it would be too late.

"I've got a hundred dollars," the old wolf had said. "I had a hundred and fifty when I was pushed out on the dodge. I've had a lot, one way and another, one time and another. But it's all gone. The gambling and the whisky and the women. And some kid-deputy is likely lying up behind a rock, somewhere on the trail ahead waiting to crack down on me and collect five thousand dollars that's on my scalp. There's nothing to all this, Lace. Nothing but grief and a bullet at the end."

Lace's thoughts were broken by appearance in the cabin door of a man who might have been Tulsa's blood-brother. The man was as squat, wide of shoulders and dark of hair and eyes and skin as Tulsa. This one said nothing. He stood looking Lace blankly up and down.

"That's Dynamite," Tulsa introduced the silent one. "Kind of a mix-up in his pedigree—a little French, a little Scotch, but mostly Blood Indian. He comes from Alberta."

57

Lace, sizing the breed, instinctively put him down as perhaps the most dangerous man, if not necessarily the most intelligent, of Tulsa's gang. He nodded to Dynamite, who acknowledged the courtesy by a brief jerk of the head, before turning back to his cooking.

During the afternoon, while Tulsa and Lace yarned of Long Riders and their ways and Dynamite hunkered against the cabin's outer wall, smoking endlessly, neither the evil-tempered Frio, nor the big, red Noisy made an appearance.

The three at the cabin ate supper.

Just before dark, Lanny, who bad been wrangling the outfit's horses, came singing along the trail. He was a looselipped, tow-haired youngster, with pale blue eyes set wide apart beneath colorless brows.

When he had eaten, Lanny went up to Lookout Rock to stand guard. Noisy came down to the cabin to eat supper and to belie his nickname. For he said not a half-dozen words during the meal. But when his greenish eyes rolled to Lace, they held something more than mere enmity, Lace thought. There was an expression of suppressed triumph about them. Frio did not come in. Nor did Tulsa express any curiosity about his failure to appear.

Tulsa seemed a little worried by Noisy's silence. He kept watch upon both Lace and the big man. And he began to talk a good deal, to brag about the hard name his bunch had, over in Utah. Lace listened without telling much of his own record, and with a small grin that Noisy seemed to find infuriating. For suddenly he leaned toward Lace.

"Of course, you hairpins down here on the Bravo Trail, you're used to so much that likely nothing anywhere here else looks big to you. But I'll tell you one thing and I'll guarantee it's straight, too—the slugs we used in Utah was just as big as any one you ever seen over here!"

"That would go for the ones the kids shoot off back East, too," Lace said thoughtfully. "So that don't seem to me to be proving a thing. Are you trying to prove something? Well, how about a game to keep the talk away? I swear! I've heard more talk about big jobs tonight than I can remember hearing in all my years on the high lines. Can anybody here play stud?"

A sudden light came into the grim, dark eyes of Dynamite. Lace saw it and grinned inwardly. The Indians and breeds he had known were usually inveterate, if not expert, gamblers. Noisy shook his head sullenly. Tulsa Jack shrugged.

"I reckon I don't mind a few hands—even with one of you 'leven footers off the Bravo Trail," he said sneeringly. "Got some cards?"

"Couple decks with the seals still on 'em, in my saddle bags," Lace informed him pleasantly. "Bought 'em in Ancho before I headed this way. I'll get 'em."

He brought in both decks and tossed them on the rough table. He grinned when Tulsa inspected both boxes carefully.

"I love a suspicious gambler," he remarked generally to the room. "It's a lot more fun to take his money off him . . . Go ahead. Open 'em up. Satisfy yourself any way you can figure out, that you've got nothing but percentages against you. Percentages, that is, plus my playing . . ."

Tulsa made a snarling noise. Noisy stared murderously at him. Dynamite was merely intent on playing. His lean, dark fingers worked and he stared at the cards as his leader dropped the first pack out of its

59

container and shuffled it.

"Take the deal," Lace suggested to Tulsa. "You're probably the oldest man here and you're certainly the homeliest. So there's no contest about it. No-limit suit you—uh—nineteen footers from the Green River? It's hard on me, the only Texas man here, but I'll bear up. And if you should happen to slip and give me a hand, I'll bear down, too."

"I hate a talking player," Tulsa said in a thick voice.

"And sometimes you can do something about it, and other times you just have to sit and sweat and suffer," Lace told him cheerfully. "Ah, well! Think of the good company you're in—all the men who wanted to do something about Lace Morrow and his aggravating ways. But couldn't quite get there . . ."

He grinned narrow-eyed at Tulsa and Noisy. Dynamite had said nothing. But he was fishing under his shirt to get out a crude money belt stitched up from tarpaulin canvas. It let a cascade of gold pieces out upon the table when he shook it. Lace put a handful of gold before him from his pockets. Tulsa wore a heavy tubular belt of leather which contained gold and some; bills. Lace looked inquiringly at Noisy.

"Still won't break the promise you made to your teacher and play with the innocents? Ah, well! Your losings are our gains I bet you. Oh! Anybody got a drink? I thought you said Lanny had been down to the Rock House . . ."

"Jug in the corner," Tulsa grunted. "Fish her out, Noisy. Five cartwheels to see your hole card. Come on!"

They anted and he dealt the cards. Noisy brought the jug and tin cups. He poured drinks for them all, and Lace, sitting with cup at his mouth, looked at

Dynamite's queen, the aces before Tulsa and himself. He drank and shook his head.

"This is the sort of suspense I never could stand. Likely, it has lost me more money at stud even than the other fellow's crooked dealing. I've just got to find out . . ."

Two twenties went out from his pile to the center. Promptly Dynamite saw the bet. A shade slowly, Tulsa pushed in his forty dollars and dealt. A king dropped on Lace's ace, a jack on Dynamite's queen, a ten on Tulsa's ace. Three twenties Lace bet this time. Dynamite saw the bet, but Tulsa shook his head.

"Got me high-carded," he grunted.

An ace came to Lace, another jack to Dynamite. Lace whistled timelessly and Dynamite stared blankly at him.

"If you've got two pair—" Lace said softly. "All right! A hundred to you, if I never see the back of my neck!"

"And fifty!" Dynamite grunted, shoving in gold.

"And a hundred," Lace drawled. "This is going to cost somebody, Alberta!"

Dynamite looked at his stack, then sidelong at Noisy. "Lend me some. Plenty. It'll cost, all right."

Noisy leaned and lifted Dynamite's hole card. Lace frowned at the pair of them and slowly Noisy put a hand behind him. He worked with a hip-pocket of his overalls and brought out a buckskin sack. Meeting Laces scowl, he began to grin unpleasantly.

"Nothing like backing up a friend," he said. "Sometimes you got to do it because he's a friend of yours. Other times it's downright pleasant to help him out. Like now . . ."

"First time I ever had a hand to be played against a whole neighborhood," Lace grunted.

Tulsa shook his head, and looked a trifle puzzled. "First time I can remember that a first hand in stud took a whole night to play," he contributed.

"All right, now!" Dynamite said snarlingly. "Here's a couple hundred more up. Maybe that pair of jacks is everything in the world I got except the clothes I set in. But it'll cost you plenty to find out."

"And two hundred," Lace drawled. "This isn't Green River. This is Lost Souls Valley. Time we get done with this hand you'll maybe want to rebrand the place, call her Lost Gold Valley. But if you learn a lot about stud, the lesson may not be too expensive. To both of you!" he added, looking up at Noisy.

Noisy's grin vanished. He watched sullenly as Dynamite pushed the remainder of his gold into the center of the table.

"Jacks!" Dynamite yelled and came erect in a tigerish movement, both hands upon the table. "I told you—"

"You'd need anyway four of'em," Lace told him calmly, without moving. "That Big Auger of yours is a wonderful dealer. Handed me three aces just when I best could use 'em."

From face to stricken face he let his eyes wander, and—"No hard feelings, I hope?" he inquired, with an edge to his voice. "I'll say one thing, here and now; there's not a thing wrong with the gambling done by such Green Riverites as last moved over here. They get a hand and they back it up to the last chip. Same as I do."

"I'm going up to the Rock," Noisy told his leader harshly. "Wonder where Frio got to? He was headed this way when I took the guard."

"Yeh, you better take the guard a spell," Tulsa nodded. "Lanny ain't much after dark—shoots too quick or not quick enough, like that time—"

He checked himself with a quick stare at the outsider in the cabin. Noisy went out, scuffing his heels like an angry man. Dynamite made a cigarette. His eyes were bloodshot and he glowered at his hands. Lace looked at the gold on the table, then at Tulsa.

"That have to conclude the session for the evening?" he inquired. "Two-handed stud's not so exciting, sometimes. But if you're in the humor for blackjack—"

"Deal it!" Tulsa grunted. "Here's fifty, Dynamite. Make it last. Not that I wouldn't have played three jacks the same as you did, at that. But we're getting kind of down . . ."

CHAPTER 10

THEY PLAYED WITH VARYING LUCK UNTIL LANNY made his appearance. Tulsa lost more often than he won, Dynamite built his pile to more than double its original size. Lanny stood over the players, fumbling with the straps of a leather money belt he wore.

"See Frio?" Tulsa asked him without taking his stare off the cards. "That crazy tomahawk ain't been down to eat or nothing."

"Seen him when I first went up to spell Noisy. He was setting on a rock by the upper trail. Didn't even look at me when I yelled at him. Had a rag around his gunhand. Deal me a hand."

"Thought you had enough blackjack down at the Rock House to do you," Tulsa said tolerantly. "You went down there with a couple hundred and come back with fifty."

"Ah, that was draw poker and setting up the drinks

for all the gals. You know me—couple weeks or so with just you homely phizzes and I got to take the curse off with a piece of calico."

"All right, then, if you want to drop your beltful, go ahead and drop her. You can have my place. I lost around a hundred and that's all I want to hand out tonight."

He got up from the table and crossed to the door. Lace dealt the cards around, playing against Dynamite's twenty and the boy's ten. He dealt the dark-faced breed a third card and Dynamite nodded and said "Fine! You're a good dealer."

"How about you, Lanny?" Lace inquired. "Comfortable?"

"Sock me—hard," Lanny grinned.

Lace dropped a ten upon the exposed four, then a three. he dealt himself a seven and grinned in his turn. "Pay twenty-one!" he announced and drew in the stakes.

Lanny took the deal and this time Dynamite played ten dollars and Lace, tiring of the game, looked at Lanny's lean pile. He put out thirty-five dollars. Lanny began to deal and both Lace and Dynamite whooped triumphantly.

"Misdeal! Pay off!" Dynamite yelled. "You never buried the top card."

Lanny pushed out the rest of his gold ruefully. Suddenly, he took from his shirt pocket a heavy, round gold locket. He held it out to Dynamite:

"Gi' me twenty on that, Dynamite," he said. "I want a chance to get square with this game. I'm feeling lucky—"

"Then I'd be a damn' fool to get you back into the game," Dynamite told him, grinning. "Uh-uh. I seen that when you come back with it. Don't want it."

"How about you, then?" The boy turned to Lace, who also shook his head, but automatically reached for the locket and opened it. "Ah, come on, now. Ain't it a pretty picture? And it's solid gold. It's easy worth twenty. But I'll take ten. I just want a chance to get square—"

Lace, staring down at the small, dark-eyed face in the old-fashioned tintype, frowned across at Lanny inquiringly.

"Give one of the gals five dollars for it," Lanny said naively. "She was lit up like a church, else she wouldn't have took it. Some feller she knows give it to her. She told me she never knew who it is, but she was lying. He took it off a gal that's down at Tull Farris' house. It ain't the gal, because I seen her and she don't look like this. It's the gal's mother."

"What do you mean, one of the men took this off the girl? What kind of a man would go around taking the picture of a girl's mother away from her?"

"Oh—I don't know the straight of it all. But there's something funny about this gal. She ain't one of the gals that dance. She just stays in Tull's house and kind of works for Bella. You know her, the big yellow-haired gal they call The Queen."

Lace nodded. Word of Bella had drifted out of the Valley and, wherever *buscaderos* swapped stories, the queen of Lost Souls Valley was familiar at least by hearsay. But this locket—and the tale that Lanny told—interested him.

"You say she's not a dance-hall girl? What's the matter with her? I never heard of any other kind around Farris'."

"Ah, she's not pretty the way the others are. I told you I seen her. Kind of skinny and white. Me, I like

65

some beef on my arm when I call a dance. This gal, you could pick her up and swing her around your head and never know you hefted a thing. But her mother, now, she's kind of pretty, ain't she? And the locket's solid gold, like I told you. Gi' me ten on it, now. And I bet you I'll show you some luck—"

But Lace found himself fascinated by that oval face and the grave, dark eyes under the widow's peak of soft hair. If the daughter had any of her mother's appearance, he thought, she would be well worth seeing. And she was a kind of servant in Tull Farris' house . . .

He asked Lanny what Long Rider had taken the locket from the girl. But Lanny had not heard, nor was he interested in the subject. He had told everything he knew: that for several weeks—three weeks, at least— the girl had been in Farris' house and was reportedly overworked and badly treated by Bella, who was next to Farris in Valley importance.

"Here's your ten," Lace told the towhead abruptly. "If you want to cut a card for it, I'm your huckleberry. But my advice is to keep it in your pocket. It's just as bad to be stony in the Valley as anywhere else."

Lanny grinned wisely and shuffled the deck. Dynamite cut the cards and pushed them to Lace, who picked a queen from the top. Lanny drew a five. He swore bitterly and looked about the room. Tulsa still loafed near the door. Lanny seemed to shrug off some thought—the idea of asking his boss for a loan, Lace decided, and shifted on the rough bench. And his mouth sagged.

Lace was caught by the boy's stiffening. He had only to turn his head, to see the blanket twitching away from one window, to face the malignant mask that was Frio's face, resting upon the stock of a carbine.

"Look out, Frio!" he yelled savagely—and as the Indian hesitated briefly, Lace slapped the candle in its bottle off the table and hurled himself sideways to the dirt floor.

He heard Frio's shot, heard the splat of the slug on the rock wall behind and above him. He had jerked his own Colt automatically as he dropped. He sent one slug in the general direction of the window, but his second and third bullets were aimed at the candle across the room, which set upon a tomato can on a box. The can rang like a bell and the cabin was in darkness.

Lace went fast and quietly the three yards to the door. Tulsa was no longer there, but whether inside or out, Lace had no way of knowing. He had not looked that way when it was light.

He paused, crouching on the doorsill. There was a moon, but it was blanketed by masses of gray cloud and only pale light filtered through. He went on to squat beyond the door, close to the cabin wall.

When a foot scuffed the hard ground before him, he tensed with pistol up. A dark shape appeared at the corner of the cabin and as soon as it was fully in sight he fired at it twice.

He was pretty sure that this was Frio, coming to the door to finish what he had bungled at the window. But if it were Tulsa or Noisy, intending to give the Indian a hand, he thought he would not be heartbroken. There was nothing about any of these hard cases from Green River to make him expect friendliness from them. If he had to fight the whole bunch now, he could hardly ask a better battlefield.

He listened to the gasping from the man fallen at the corner. It was quickly over. He looked behind him, but nobody showed. So he stood and edged toward the moveless figure on the ground.

It was Frio, fallen across his Winchester. He was dead. Sure of this, Lace looked behind him again, then called to the others, "All right! Make up a light. Your feather duster's finished—through."

He went back to the door. And Tulsa appeared, coming from the opposite corner of the cabin. Across the width of the door, the two men looked at each other. The light was too pale to show shades of expression, but Tulsa said calmly enough, "Got him, did you? Well, when a man starts out to bushwhack another man and gets hisself shot to pieces, I always figure he got what he ought've expected."

"Fair enough!" Lace conceded. "The rest of the bunch likely to take it that way, too? Noisy, in particular?"

"Frio was nobody's special sidekick, if that's what you mean. Noisy just don't like you. Not because you knocked Frio around this morning, but because he don't like your style."

A match flared inside and once more the candle was lighted. Tulsa went in and Lace trailed him, still holding his pistol along his leg. But Dynamite only blinked at him and Lanny, picking up the second candle from the floor, stared almost open-mouthed at Lace.

"All right with you?" Lace demanded of Dynamite.

The breed shrugged with blank face. He said in what seemed to be an honestly careless tone, "In a case like that, a man kills his own snakes. He was the one that chose you. If he couldn't get there, it was his hard luck. Yeh, all right with me."

"Same here!" Lanny said importantly, then turned very red when the others laughed.

Dynamite crossed the room and went out. Lace moved to where lie had his back to a wall. Suddenly,

68

Tulsa shifted position and with thumb hooked in his shell belt he stared at the door. He was frowning. Lanny gaped at him, then at the door. While Lace watched, wondering what had come into the boss' mind, Dynamite came inside. He stopped short and looked at Tulsa.

"Don't start worrying till you need to," he said. "I got his belt and the regular split is all I ever asked for. You can take your hand off your pistol, Tulsa."

He went on to the table and put his hand under his shirt. Tulsa, Lace observed, did not relax until another home-made canvas belt was spilling gold upon the tabletop. Then he went to stand beside Dynamite. They counted the money.

"Two hundred and twenty," Tulsa said at last. "Split four ways, that's fifty-five a share. Reckon we can give Lanny full share out of that—and he can pile most of the rocks over Frio come morning, huh? Farris'll buy Frio's horse and outfit."

"Sounds fair enough," Dynamite nodded. "I'll take Noisy up his share when I relieve him on guard."

"How about you standing a guard, Morrow?" Tulsa inquired of Lace, turning. "Seems fair enough for you—"

"Nothing fair about it," Lace disagreed, very calmly. "I drifted back to the Valley on some business of my own. The Valley belongs to Tull Farris and he runs it his own way. One of his conditions, for letting the like of your bunch hang out here, is keeping the door watched. Somebody has to be on guard there all the time, so long as a Long Rider's around."

He shifted position and yawned. "If you hadn't been here, somebody else would have been watching the in-trail. I wouldn't have been expected to. Me, I'm what you call a visitor right now. If I settle down, I'll take my share of guard. Uh-uh! You didn't cut me in for a share of what Frio was packing—and I had as much right to it as anybody else. If it hadn't been for me you wouldn't be counting the gold now. So you can stand your own guard."

Tulsa lowered at him. Dynamite's face was blank.

"More and more, I can figure up things I don't like about you," Tulsa said grimly. "We'll maybe talk about that, later on, farther down the Valley."

"Any time you feel big and snorty," Lace shrugged. "Dynamite, when you see Noisy, you tell him the straight of what hit Frio and say I'm an unusual light sleeper. He might want to be thinking about that tonight, when he comes off guard . . . ."

CHAPTER 11

When the five of them rode deeper into the Valley next morning, Lace found his thoughts casting ahead, rather than back to where a cairn of rocks covered the dead Frio.

One of Tull Farris' men, a lanky, silent man of middle age, had appeared before dawn to take the guard from Tulsa's bunch. He had said only that Tull wanted the newcomers down at the Rock House and had gone on to Lookout Rock to send Dynamite in. He had looked at each man curiously, no more so at Lace than at any other.

Lace and Lanny brought up the drag of the riders on the narrow trails that threaded the boulder-studded floor of the Valley. The boy talked incessantly. Sometimes Lace listened, more often he speculated about the task

70

he had set himself. Occasionally he recalled the gold locket that now sagged in his shirt pocket and wondered who the girl might be.

Some painted charmer of the dance-halls, doubtless. There would be a simple explanation of her servant-work in Farris' house. But recollection of the clear, grave face of that girl's mother, as it appeared in the locket picture, made him curious about the daughter. Whatever else the pictured woman might have been, Lace thought, there was not a line of coarseness, of commonness, about her features. He was anxious to see this girl.

Quite a few men were in the Valley now, Lanny informed him. Chick Haynes' bunch was at the Rock House, resting after a hard and unsuccessful raid into Mexico. Gano Brown's gang was there too. Seven men, or, counting the two leaders, nine.

"I only seen one man of Tull Farris'," Lanny told Lace. "But, of course, he's got more working for him. Some are due in any time, from what I heard."

"I reckon," Lace agreed dryly, and in his mind there was the picture of Tull Farris, lank, murderous, cunning. "Barto Awe's not in the Valley, huh?"

"Barto Awe? No, I never heard anybody speak about him. "Is he one of the big boys?"

"In a way," Lace told him. "One of the biggest . . ."

He put more questions during the slow ten miles they rode. But Lanny had heard no more of the Pluma robbery than of Barto Awe. Either the regulars at the Rock House had not wanted to talk before a strange kid, or—

Lace mulled it over. In a way, Barto Awe was Tull Farris' closest associate. It was not friendship in any sense of the word. They were merely "business associates" of the Long Rider persuasion. But they were very close. So any thought of Barto Awe brought natural thought of Tull Farris. For Tull was the unquestioned boss of Lost Souls Valley, shrewd schemer of raids on which he never rode. He took his cut from everybody's spoils—and eventually most of the remainder found its way into his pocket, because the Long Riders drank and gambled and danced in the Rock House he owned.

It's a blame' boggy ford, Lace told himself, staring straight ahead and ignoring Lanny's gossip about Bella, who was said to hate the pale, slender girl who did her chores, Blame' boggy! If Barto pulled the Pluma job, you'd expect to find him right here in the Valley on a spree. And, it seems he's not. I wonder where he really is . . . And I wonder if Tull was the brain behind the Pluma business . . .

He shook his head at last. There seemed to be no answer to the question—none—except in the Rock House.

A man came out of a side trail, where the Valley widened, a smallish man, dark, big-nosed, with quick, narrow blue eyes. He stared at Lace Morrow, then jerked his arm aloft and rammed the spurs to his big buckskin and pounded down upon him. Lace grinned at Tom Elton and when the buckskin was whirled deftly, they banged each other upon the backs and cursed one another fluently and affectionately.

"You old son of a what-you-may-call-it!" Lace told the little outlaw at the end, regarding him with head upon one side. "You don't change a bit. *Amor de dios*! You must be a hundred-and-fifty now. But I swear you don't look a day over a hundred—just as plain ugly as you ever did look. How come nobody's wiped you off the earth for the good of the country?"

Tom Elton replied in kind and they jogged along stirrup-to-stirrup exchanging gossip of Long Riders they both knew. But when Lace dropped the first word about the Pluma job, it was as if a curtain had dropped between him and Elton. Tom shrugged.

"Sounded like a pretty neat job, except for the useless killings. Yeh, pretty neat, way we heard the tale."

"You mean it wasn't done by somebody out of the Valley?" Lace demanded in a surprised voice—and made his expression match his tone. "Why, that'd be funny. Strangers coming into Farris' bailiwick and doing a job and nobody among the regulars knowing about it!"

"Do'no'," Tom Elton evaded the question uncomfortably.

When Lace persisted in discussing the oddities of the Pluma job, Tom at last made an exasperated gesture. "Listen, Lace," he said almost pleadingly, "if there's anything you want to know, why'n't you wait and ask Tull? You better ask him about anything or everything. Do that, will you now? As a favor to an old sidekick."

Lace, staring with the proper appearance of bewilderment, wondered if any news of his parole could possibly have got "on the grapevine." If so, Lace Morrow would not long enjoy that immunity granted by the Governor. But mentally he shook his head. It was hardly possible that anyone in the Valley had become informed. Something else explained Tom Elton's manner with an old *companero* of the secret trails. He shrugged fatalistically and told himself that he had expected this to be a hard job. So nothing that might happen should surprise him.

"Why, if there's some reason for not talking, we

won't say a word!" he told Tom. "But I didn't know it was special . . ."

They came to the place where the Valley opened into a natural amphitheater—precisely as a gourd swells at its base.

A dozen buildings were sprawling across the width of the wider space, cabins of log or natural rock. In the foreground was the long bulk of the Rock House, where Tull Farris lived and maintained dance-hall and saloon and gambling tables. It was all very familiar to Lace. Nothing seemed changed, not even the woman in a bright red dress, walking toward Rock House. But Tom Elton grunted suddenly. He looked with something like the old carelessness toward Lace. "New, since you was here last. Bella, the big gal the boys call the Queen of Lost Souls Valley. Tull's notion of what a bolt of calico ought to be. Reckon, though, she feels her nose to be kind of out of joint these days, with that other gal, Marian, up the hill."

"I heard something like that," Lace said easily and with some truth. "Tull's kind of gone on Marian, huh?"

"Reckon. When Topeka and that Mex', Delgado, brought her in, Tull put her in the little cabin off at the end, yonder—one old Lobo Sands died in that time, remember? And he won't let none of the boys bother her, either."

"Where'd Topeka and Lucio pick her up?"

Lace kept his tone to the same note of casualness. Tom seemed not to notice that he was being pumped. He said easily, "If anybody knows, it's them—and Tull, of course. But nobody outside of the, three seems to know. Not even Bella. She wants Marian turned out of the Valley. When Tull told her to shut up, she wasn't a bit pleased. Started on the liquor and hit it up hard.

74

Bella ain't used to taking second seat from nobody. She liked the idea of being queen around here."

They crossed the distance—already spanned by Tulsa and Dynamite and Lanny and Noisy—to the front of the Rock House. Tom Elton gestured toward the corner.

"Same old place to put Plata—and it'll be like old times to see him back there in a stall, *por dios*! Hope you stick a while, Lace. Put Plata away and go on in to see Tull. Ought to be a hen on big enough to need a man with your record!"

Lace grinned by way of farewell to the ugly, likable little man and rode the familiar path to Tull Farris' stable. Nobody was there, but there were horses in the several stalls. He had to ride the length of the long shed to find a place for Plata. When he had unsaddled and fed the gray and come back into the open, Tull Farris himself stood in the back door of the Rock House. He looked steadily at Lace, then suddenly grinned. "Certainly good to see a man that got back his sense!" he greeted him. "Come on in, fella. Nothing much's changed. Nothing than other a smokeroo out of Smoky Hill's crowd, anyhow."

Lace returned the grin and crossed to the *buscaderos'* brain to put out his hand and grip the long, freckled paw of Farris. They looked each other up and down openly, grinned again and went into the big kitchen of the house. A withered Mexican woman turned her masklike face as she worked over a big range. Lace called her Concha and she showed her gums in a broad smile.

He went on, with Tull Farris, into the adjoining room, which was behind the long bar-room and gambling-place. Tull yelled for "Ikey" and a bow-legged man came in. He was a stranger to Lace, but apparently Lace Morrow of the famous old Smoky Hills gang was no

75

stranger to him. For he called Lace by name and said he was glad to meet him.

"Bring us a quart of the real quill," Tull ordered. "I don't see many of the Lace Morrow kind drifting in— ain't many left, I reckon. Let's see . . . Smoky got rubbed out in that bushwhacking up on the Canadian. Old Crow Ed collected the wrong end of a shotgun in Gunnison. And—"

He recounted the bloody ends of the Smoky Hills bunch before the little bartender came back with the quart. They filled their glasses, Tull in his big half-barrel chair, Lace hunkered against a rock wall. Ceremoniously, they drank.

"I reckon we know part of your tale," Tull said as he poured the second drink for them. "That part about the charge of robbery and you getting twenty years and busting away from Roy Jacks. But after that—well, you kind of drug some smoke over your trail. But I said to Tom Elton: You just wait. Old Lace'll pop into my Valley one of these days. He will that! Once they slept in the Valley, they always came back—if not too weighted down with a bunch of lead. How about it?"

He lifted his glass, a lean and wolfish man of something more than middle age, wiry-looking, with the toughness of whipcord and whalebone and whangleather strings about him. Lace set himself to match wits with the shrewdest brain he had ever known along the high lines.

"Roy Jacks is on what he figures is a hot trail, right now. Yes, sir! He's on Barto Awe's trail for that Pluma job."

Tull stared with a puzzled expression. "You—you sure of that, Lace? I hadn't heard word about it. I certainly hadn't. Where'd you get the tale?"

Lace shrugged. He put down his cup and began to make a cigarette, quite conscious that Tull's narrowed eyes were steady upon him.

"When I doubled back from the Coast—I'd laid it on thick to Roy Jacks about heading for the northern range and I thought this country would be my safest hide-out—I slid into Darien to get Plata and my outfit off a friend who'd been keeping everything for me. And I got kind of reckless, maybe. Anyhow, I slid over to Pluma after dark and when I happened to notice a light in the sheriff's office, I went over and listened at the window."

He flicked a match against his thumbnail, set the tiny flame to his cigarette and drew in smoke. "Roy Jacks was talking over the Pluma job with the district attorney. I knew a little about the business, for it was all the talk around where I'd stopped on the way back from Frisco. Nobody seemed to know, exactly, who had pulled the job, but it had all the earmarks of Barto Awe, to my notion. And it seems Roy Jacks has got something in the way of proof—something he thinks is proof enough, anyway. he told the district attorney that when he'd done two things he'd be ready to get beat for reelection. "When he heels Barto Awe and watches him kick for those murders, and when he gets me to the pen to do my twenty years, he'll call it a day."

It amused him to think that a good deal of this was actual truth and that Tull Farris, suspicious as any born liar is suspicious of what he hears, would have to admit that it was truth. Which would naturally tend to confuse him about the imaginary suspicion of Roy Jacks, that Barto Awe was his man for the bank-robbery and murders.

"Roy Jacks is a dang' good sheriff," Tull said between his teeth. "Too good to be let stay alive . . ."

"I was mightily grateful to the boys for the money that paid my lawyers," he said. "Even if no lawyers alive could have got me out of that mess in Pluma."

"Tom Elton and some of the others was ready to do more'n that," Tull assured him. "They was all organized to ride down to Pluma some moonlight night and rope Roy Jacks' jail and pull her up by the roots and shake you out of it. Even if you had cut stick from the Valley and the old ways and turned a dang' nester. Then we heard how Roy Jacks had got worried and started you fast for Huntsville. Next word was when you tied Jacks up in a pullman berth and hightailed. What happened?"

Lace told his story briefly and at the end, mindful of the effect he must produce here, he hardened face and eyes. "Roy Jacks is not the officer I would pick to chase me. He's too dang' much like a bulldog with a strong streak of bloodhound in him. I tell you, when I had him under a gun in that Frisco park I was as near as I've ever been to killing a man just to kill him."

"Too bad you never done it! Too dang' bad!" There was no alteration in the lean, brown face, but Tull Farris' eyes shone like bits of metal. "I say, you can't be too squeamish! If a man bodaciously pushes himself into your road and won't stay out—finish him! You know what Billy the Kid used to say: There's some folks that nothing but killing 'em will ever teach 'em to keep their noses into their own business. *Por dios*! That goes for more places than Lincoln County, or New Mexico. It goes for the wide world, far's I've traveled. Roy Jacks is got to be settled."

He held out his hand for Lace's cup, caught it deftly and filled it splashing full. Lace leaned to accept it. He grinned.

"You don't expect to get an argument out of me, I

hope, about rubbing out Roy Jacks' mark? You see, Tull, I've been on the dodge a long time, first and last. I've noticed that the man the John Laws are set against are the killers. So even if I had the leaning toward killing that I never have had, I'd think it poor business to do it. But if you can show me Roy up against me in a fair fight, I'll get him before he gets me. If I can. And that reminds me!"

He drank, staring with a small frown across his cup at Tull.

CHAPTER 12

WHILE HE SAT LOWERING AT THE FAR WALL, A VOICE rose in the bar-room. A woman's voice, loud, but in its lazy, husky note not at all unpleasant. Lace turned a little but could not see the speaker. Tull seemed to observe his curiosity, though he had not moved a muscle.

"That's Bella," he explained. "She's kind of sore at the world right now, and she's hitting the bottle too hard. I'll have to bow my neck with her, I reckon, and pop her back to where she belongs. She could easy be a nuisance."

Then he turned to face Lace directly. "Funny, me not hearing about Roy Jacks thinking Barto pulled the Pluma job! What about this bank fella they got in jail? Wes Kincaid? What does Roy Jacks figure him for— somebody hooked to Barto Awe? The man that staked out the job?"

Lace grinned amusedly. "That, from what I could hear and piece together, is just Roy's idea of being smart. The way he talked to the district attorney, they

79

did figure it that way at first. And when they got this new notion they thought it was better to keep Kincaid in his cage, to fool the li'l birdies still outside. He won't figure in the case a-tall. They don't believe he had a thing to do with it. And that is just—too—bad . . ."

Tull watched him frowningly. Lace stared grimly at the floor until Tull said, "How's that? Why's it too bad?"

"Because Kincaid's the nephew of Judge Bettencourt! And Bettencourt's the man who sentenced me to twenty years for a job I didn't even know about. Besides, Kincaid's supposed to marry a girl the judge thinks a sight more of than he thinks of his own nephew! If Roy Jacks had gone on with his first notion, if he'd took Kincaid into court before the kind of jury that tried me in Pluma—well, Bettencourt wouldn't feel so high and mighty about upholding the law, and all that!"

He kept his own face in an ugly mask while he studied the stony features of Tull Farris. If Tull were for any reason suspicious of him, Lace thought that he had him puzzled now.

He wondered what Tom Elton was doing in the Valley these days. Certainly, Tom's evasive way with him, an old friend, indicated something moving under the surface. But then he reminded himself that Curly Camp would be riding into the Valley very soon now. And there was a salty hairpin, the kind who would make you a good friend and a bad enemy, the kind a man could trust with his life. He shrugged.

"Well," he told Tull, "here I am, right back where I was before I tried to be an honest rancher. I own Plata and his rigging and a couple of handfuls of steel. When I put my hat on, the roof's all shingled. I'm ready for something. This Tulsa Jack, that I rode down with, told me you sent him word you had a hen on. What have you got that I can take a hand in? I reckon I don't have to remind you about my record . . ."

"Not a thing for you right now," Tull answered absently. "I wonder what's in Roy Jacks' mind, to make him suspicion Barto Awe on that Pluma job? Blazes! If Barto had done that one, I'd certainly know about it. 'Course I would! And Barto's clean up above Guadalupe. He's on a little cow-deal up there that I schemed out for him. Ah, hell! If he had done that Pluma job he couldn't fool me. I'd know about it."

Abruptly, he looked with something like challenge at Lace, who was still playing the part of a grim man thinking about his hatred, staring moodily at the wall.

"You're no friend of Barto Awe!" Tull said belligerently.

"Who said I was? Barto's a crazy killer. And when he rubbed out Bob Vardon from behind, I would have handed him some lead poisoning he'd have died from. He knew that well enough, and he knew he didn't want to tangle with Lace Morrow! If I come up against Barto and he rubs me a little bit the wrong way, I'll show him the quick draw and the sudden shoot. But if you're hinting that I'd tie in with a sheriff to snag Barto, that's something else. I'd bear up if I heard Barto had passed in his checks from a gut-shot, yelling himself to death. But as for helping Roy Jacks—"

He got up and now he was grinning pleasantly. "It's like this, Tull. Roy Jacks is naturally on the other side of our fence, being a sheriff. He's an honest sheriff, too. He runs with the hounds and nobody else. You've tried to make arrangements with him and you know what happened to the men that did the hinting for you. You tried to put some burrs under his saddle blanket and get

81

him bucked out of that sheriff's office. And you know what happened to the nitwits you sent on the job—one's still in the pen and one's certainly still dead. Maybe every man's got his price, maybe Roy's got his price. But it certainly is some price you can't pay."

He wagged a finger at Farris. "All right. What I'm saying is, Roy is too good a sheriff for us to be comfortable around. He's on my trail and he won't call off the dogs until he gets me—or something. Naturally, I'm against him. And, quaint as that makes it seem, I'm for Barto Awe when he's bucking the law. But there's another side of the tale. It won't make a bit of difference to Roy Jacks, whether Barto did that useless killing in Pluma. There's plenty to swing Barto on, that can be proved. But Barto's not going to be caught. Killed, maybe, but not caught. And when he starts smoking it with Roy Jacks, maybe both of'em will get rubbed out. So, either way, whether Roy downs Barto, or Barto downs Roy, or they down each other—fine!"

A tall, very shapely blonde woman in red came into the room from the bar-room. She stopped, leaning against the door to look Lace Morrow up and down from hat to boots. She was somewhere in her middle twenties and, as Lanny had remarked, she was unusually pretty, if in a hard, calculating fashion.

"Your taste in calico is certainly getting a lot better," Lace told Tull Farris, with jerk of head toward the woman.

"I could give you a big argument about that," Tull said sourly. "That's Bella. The boys call her—"

"Queen of Lost Souls Valley," she finished for him, still looking at Lace. "And you're the famous Lace Morrow, the last man out of the Smoky Hills bunch . . . Tom Elton and some of the other old-timers have told me a lot about you. And I heard a little more just a while back, from the gang you rode in with. They say you're hell on wheels, *hombre*. Tull says so, too."

"Raised on barb' wire and dynamite and cowtown whisky," Lace told her, grinning. "Cut my teeth on a pair of hoglegs. But you mustn't take that Green River crowd except with salt. Lots of things look mighty big to men from the short grass."

"Come on out to the bar and I'll let you buy me a drink. If I like you as much as I think I'm going to, maybe you can squander away a lot of that money you took off the hard cases from Utah. Come along! I'll make Tull jealous and that'll make him happy. He's a curly wolf when he gets mad."

Tull grinned, but only absently. Behind his own amused expression, Lace was wondering what undercurrent ran there. He sensed more than the woman's words seemed to say. Then thought came of the girl Marian, of the locket he now owned.

"Never heard of Tull getting jealous when the drinks jingled his cash drawer," he told Bella. "But even if it got me killed, it would probably be worth it. Come along, *Bonita*! I have got se-ve-ral twenties that used to weigh down the famous tough outfit from the Green River. We'll blow some of it getting better acquainted. Tull, if you happen to miss us later on, you'll know that she's kidnaped a pore cowboy that was too weak to resist even if he'd wanted to—or the other way around. Look for us up around Dallas or Sa'ton'. We—"

Interruption came. Through the door from the kitchen a small figure came running, a girl in a faded plaid skirt and a patched shirt of gray flannel, obviously a man's shirt and far too large for her slender body. She was very pale and seemed all eyes to Lace, as, with a start, he recognized her resemblance to the picture in the locket he had won from Lanny.

She ran across the room to Tull Farris and seemed to be sheltering herself behind him while she looked fearfully at the door through which she had entered. Bella was close to Lace. He felt her arm stiffen against his.

"What's the matter with you?" Bella demanded huskily, and her face was suddenly very red. "Talk up, you—!"

"Shut up, Bella," Tull commanded in an even tone. "Now, Marian, what's the trouble?"

"I—I was coming from my cabin to the kitchen and a man jumped out from behind one of the other cabins and grabbed at me. He tore my sleeve—see! And I ran. But he followed me clear up to the door. He almost caught me. I never saw him before. He—he jumped out at me, that's all."

"Well, for—sake!" Bella cried furiously. "Almost touched you, did he? Now, ain't that just the awfulest thing anybody ever heard about? You're too grand to be touched I suppose? And maybe that's why you set in that window of yours the blessed day long and ogle the boys passing by? Because you don't want'em playing in your flower bed . . . You make me so sick and tired I—I Get back into that kitchen, you hear me? Get back there!"

"I don't sit in the window ogling anybody! And I'm not going back out there if that man's still waiting," Marian flared at the older woman. "I haven't spoken to any man in the Valley except when I had to. And I'm not going—"

Bella moved quickly—too fast to be stopped by Lace, even if he had wanted to interfere, too fast to be checked by Tull Farris before her open palm had slapped Marian across the cheek and staggered the girl. She struck at Marian again.

"You little—" she said huskily, almost gasping. "You come in here and try to pull something over my eyes! You think you're setting pretty—you can hand me backtalk! I'll break that skinny neck of yours! I'll—"

Marian cowered against the wall with arms protecting her face. Tull Farris moved before Bella had struck the girl again. He caught Bella by the arm and jerked her around, then sent her staggering against Lace.

"Let her alone or I'll break your neck!" he snarled at Bella. "As for that fella that grabbed at you, Marian—"

He moved grimly toward the kitchen. Bella, leaning upon Lace, but apparently unconscious of it, screamed after Tull.

"You come back here! Let the—get out and scratch gravel with the rest of us; let her take care of herself! Serve her right if one of the boys does grab her—for all she tries to act like she'd mind it. She would—like blazes! She—"

But Tull was gone and from beyond the kitchen his angry voice sounded. "You git and do it fast! And if ever you lift a finger at that kid again, you won't last as long in my Valley as the celluloid cat in blazes, you hear me? If you want to snatch girls, go around to the dance-hall and talk to girls that understand your language! Git!"

He came back and grinned at the slender, black-haired girl who still leaned against the wall, the red imprint of Bella's palm upon one thin check.

"It's all right now, Marian," he told her. "That fella's gone and he ain't likely to bother you again, either. If he does, you tell me—and that one time more'll be his last!"

"Ah, let's go buy that drink!" Bella snarled at Lace. "I need something to take the taste of that out of my mouth!"

"See you some more, Lace," Tull called. "You're sticking around, of course, and we'll do some figuring. Likely, there's a hen we can put on."

"What about the one you told Tulsa you're figuring?"

"Now, now! Don't crowd me.. I've got to figure everything. Wasn't for me, more of you boys'd be doing the cottonwood prance or dying off from powder burns. But it's Tull Farris, *por dios*! that schemes things so they go off like a clock. And the reason my schemes work is because I won't let nobody crowd me and won't let nobody crowd into a place where maybe he's not the man for it. Go ahead and keep Bella quiet. We'll scheme one for you."

Lace nodded carelessly and slid an arm through Bella's. She smiled up at him mechanically, but as they went out into the long bar-room he saw her looking furtively back.

He wondered what she saw to make her scowl. In his turn, he looked that way. He decided that it was what Bella had failed to see that irritated her. For neither Tull nor Marian was in sight. Bella muttered to herself. Then, catching Lace's eyes inquiringly upon her, she smiled at him again, the mechanical lip-stretching of the woman of pleasure.

"Handsomeness, I'm certainly glad you showed up!" she told him—and there was sincerity in her voice. "Is that good enough for you—that I'm glad you're here?"

"I always did believe that plenty ought to be enough for anybody," he assured her smilingly. "What more could I want, in Lost Souls Valley, than to have the queen of the shebang glad to see me?"

They stopped at the bar and Lace looked down it to the men congregated at the far end. Tulsa, Dynamite, Noisy and Lanny stood beside Gano Brown and four or five of Brown's men. Lace knew the hulking redhead from the old days, but they had never been close acquaintances. He jerked a hand up and Brown nodded genially. Then Ike brought a bottle.

CHAPTER 13

AS THEY DRANK, LACE WATCHED EVERYTHING IN THE barroom. He had no reason to expect trouble from Gano Brown or Chick Haynes. Both would know his record, and if Tull Farris accepted him now neither leader was likely to object. But there was a sort of tension about the Long Riders gathered with Brown and Tulsa Jack.

"When'd you come into the Valley?" he asked Bella, more to make talk than because he cared to know. "Used to be we never saw a pretty girl this side of Ancho or Pluma."

"Going on two years. I was in Dallas, dancing in a honkatonk, when Tull drifted in. You know how he looks when he's on a spree—all clothes and diamonds. Well, when he walked in looking like all the ready money in Texas, and began to tell me about a cow-town where I could knock 'em loose from their rolls, I listened. And here I landed and—here I am!"

"Who's that kid that's making all the trouble? She something pretty new in your life?"

"Ah!" she snarled."Gi' me back that bottle. It takes a bunch of straight whisky to get that taste out of my mouth. Tull makes me so sick and tired I—I—"

She filled her glass to the rim and jerked it up like a man. She drank it like a man, too, without sputtering. The glass rapped the bar and she scowled blankly straight ahead.

"Always favoring her! Tull is, I mean. If I had my way, I'd take the living hide off her with a bull-whip. Mealy-mouthed! Pretends she's too good to mix with the boys. Won't let one within a hundred yards of her, but she's got to come howling to Tull. And he backs her up! He's called just about every man in the Valley over her."

She poured another drink and held it. Her red mouth was curled scornfully. She shrugged and tossed off the whisky. "I was a Number Nine Nitwit ever to pull up stakes and come down here because Tull had a slick tongue. I ought to've called in a couple of the boys at the honkatonk when he first showed up there and rolled him into the alley and cleaned him out. Here I am, stuck in this hole, can't leave it. And on top of that he comes ramming that—down my neck."

Ike moved down the bar and reached for the quart. She slapped the bartender's hand away and drew the bottle toward her.

"Don't go sneaking off with that!" she snarled. "Gawd knows whisky's about the only friend a gal's got in this forsaken place. Come on, Lace. Let's take a table and settle down and do some serious drinking. From the tale, you was in Frisco when you got sheriff-trouble and hit back this way. Frisco . . . I was there, once. And what I wouldn't give to hear the cable-cars come jangling up California Street Hill on a foggy night, and walk into Zinkand's or Bonini's Manger or the Poodle Dog!"

She caught his arm, smiling up at him.

"Come on over and talk. I've got two empty ears!"

Lace returned her smile. He wondered if he could get her drunk enough to be off guard, so that she would answer certain questions he wanted to ask. He looked again at the men standing down the bar.

Tulsa and Noisy had turned slightly, so that they could watch Lace and Bella. They were smiling, and it seemed to Lace that the smiles were oddly malicious—and pleased as well. But when Bella, hand on Lace's arm, began to move him toward the table, leaning close and smiling up into his face, both of the Green River men lost their smiles. They seemed puzzled.

Tulsa shifted position so that he looked at Gano Brown. He said something to Brown and the big redhead turned to stare at Lace and scowl uncertainly. Then he shrugged a heavy shoulder and across the room his grunt carried audibly.

"Dang' if I know, exactly. But just you-all wait. That's all. Just wait and see."

Lace kept the quart at Bella's elbow and indicated it frequently while she talked aimlessly and constantly about all manner of things large and small. She drank steadily and seemed not to notice that Lace's glass did not often go to the bottle. She told him about the places where she had danced, the towns she had seen, the men she had known.

"Reno, Nevada, now," she said thickly. "There was a town for you. Sky was the limit on everything. Money everywhere you turned. We made it and we blowed it. Everybody made it and everybody blowed it. Reno was a grand place . . ."

Lace, studying her while he mulled over all the cross-currents and tangles he had noticed since coming into the Valley, drew her skillfully back to her grievances.

89

"And after having all that, here you are in a two-bit joint, a girl with looks and brains and all. That's not so good, *Bonita*. And, too—Well, you know what I mean, that kid sort of knocking your horns off . . ."

She swore viciously, blue eyes very bright and hard. She poured another drink and gulped it and pounded her fist on the table. Lace nodded sympathetically.

"What's it about her? That's what I want to know. What's it about that skinny, black-haired kid with her goggle eyes and her whining? She got something I ain't got? She got half what I've got? Tell me that!"

"Not half what you've got," he assured her. "What tangles me, though, is why you stand it! Why don't you pack her back to wherever she's from?"

"Yeh! Why don't I? Because I can't! She's Tull's idee of what he wants, right now. And nobody else can open his mouth about it. He's going to shove me out, now I've been here all this time. That's what he's figuring on. Going to push me out and make her the queen of the Valley."

"Where'd he pick up a kid like that?" Lace inquired, keeping his voice casual, facing her almost blankly.

"Back over in the hills somewheres. Topeka Cates and that swell-up Mex', Delgado, brought her in about three weeks ago. I don't know what was behind it or where Tull bought in on it in the first place. What the blazes does it matter? She's here and she's going to stay and—"

She poured another drink and filled Lace's glass. They drank and she put a round, white arm upon the table and rested her yellow head upon it. She looked at Lace and smiled loosely. He caught her hand under the table and her fingers closed upon his.

The men at the bar were entirely too interested in Lace

90

Morrow and his companion, Lace told himself. They were constantly turning sideways for furtive, curious glances. There was strain in the air very evident to one so sensitive as Lace Morrow. He wondered if it were his monopolizing of Tull Farris' girl that tensed them; if they expected Tull to make violent objection . . .

"I like you—lots," Bella said slowly, blurrily. "You're the kind I could go for in a big way. I'm just drunk enough to make a fool of myself and tell you. But maybe I'm cooked enough to see something I wouldn't notice sober . . ."

"And what's that?" Lace inquired, with a mechanical grin. For he was watching Gano Brown and Tulsa and the others. "My particular style of good looks, maybe?"

"Uh-uh . . . The kind of guy you really are, under that face of yours. Hard and kind of cold. You think things over before you jump. And when you do jump, it's probably straight at somebody. You never have bothered around with women, much. I get the idee that's because you don't like'em. You think they're all right in their place but you don't need much of'em. You'd rather be around with men."

"And not even a li'l' bitsy tea leaf!" Lace cried mockingly. "She just sits and looks at a man and reaches in and takes out his insides. There he is! The old tintype and no mistake. All right! I never have monkeyed around women much. Never had the time for'em. I don't think they're good friends the way a man is. I never in my life saw a woman who had what a man would call a real friend. But I like'em—in their place. In their place they're fine. Now—"

She continued to stare with that sleepwalker fixity at him. There had been a time when Bella of Lost Souls Valley was beautiful; no arguing that. Even now she

91

was far more attractive than ninety-nine out of every hundred dance-hall girls to be found in cow-towns. Clever? Lace wondered.

"Gano Brown and Chick Haynes are here," he said slowly, as if thinking aloud. "Wonder when Barto Awe is coming in? Happen to know, Bella?"

Without raising her cheek from her arm, she said, "Do'no'. From things I've heard, he's no friend of yours. Didn't happen to come back to the Valley looking for him, did you Lace? To—settle off the old score?"

Lace laughed and moved his empty glass about. "Barto's the world's worst poker-player—and esteems himself to be one of the best," he told her carelessly. "I don't know of a combination I'd rather buck. Barto gets the fun and the practice, while I collect the money to spend on Bellas. And with all the jobs Barto's been doing, he ought to be loaded down with *dinero* now. You didn't hear when he's coming in?"

"Not a word," she denied. "No, never a word."

He was looking straight at her and now he saw the change in her blue eyes. Blurriness and softness went out of them. It startled him to see live, bright, unfriendly intelligence turned his way from those eyes which an instant before had been hazed by liquor. It was—he told himself—like watching a wet rag drawn over a dirty windowpane. One moment she was drunk, the next cold sober.

She drummed long fingers upon the table and smiled at him in a way he didn't like. "Smart boy!" she said drawlingly. "Gets a pore dance-hall floozie cockeyed and pumps out of her everything she knows. What did I say about you, Lace Morrow? Cold and hard inside, under a nice grin. Fella, you could fool a lot of women and you could certainly fool most of the men. But not Bella—not any."

"What are you talking about?" he countered, staring. "I asked you a simple question and you—what's it talking, the hooch? Who's trying to fool you?"

"I know all about Barto giving it to your side-kick, Bob Vardon, in the back. I know the word you sent to Barto, then. I heard you talking to Tull out back, about how you feel. Like you'd cooled off now, and didn't want to rub Barto out."

She lifted her face and sat laughing at him. "You can handle your face good, even your hands and your voice. But you can't talk about Barto Awe and keep what you really think from showing in your eyes, fella. You didn't fool me, even if you fooled Tull. You came back here looking for Barto Awe, figuring on rubbing him out. That's all you came for, is my guess. And you want to know—I don't know why, but you want to know—if it was Barto and his bunch that pulled the Pluma job. You dragged it in when you talked to Tull. You thought I'd get pie-eyed and spill something. No, you never fooled me a bit. You kind of got fooled yourself!"

She pushed back her chair and with hands flat on the table lifted herself. She was unsteady when she stood, but perfectly clear of mind, he thought savagely. She lifted one hand from the table and waggled a forefinger at him.

"I don't know what you think you're after in the Valley. I don't know why you're talking about the Pluma job—"

"Was I talking about any particular job?" he interrupted, grinning up at her. "I thought I asked you if Barto was due back soon, if you knew when he's coming in. Bella, you're cockeyed. You're hitting it too

93

strong, these days. That kid has got you on the run and you're trying to drown your sorrows. And that never got anybody anywhere."

He got up and smiled tolerantly at her. "You ought to throw the bottle out of the window for a while. Try it, now! I'm just talking for your good."

CHAPTER 14

LACE WATCHED HER TURN AND GO STAGGERING TOWARD the back room in which Tull Farris should be.

"Might've known she'd turn out to be a copper-riveted tank," he told himself irritably. "And she'll carry that tale to Tull and he'll think it over."

Then, catching sight of the faces turned his way from the bar, he grinned faintly and moved over to stand before the hulking, red-headed Gano Brown.

"Long time no see you, Gano," he said cheerfully.

"Long time," Brown agreed, nodding.

"I just happened to notice you boys eyeing us," Lace went on, in good-humored tone. "What was all the watching about? Not supposed to be etiquette maybe, to buy Bella her drinks? Tull likely to paint up for war?"

Gano shrugged without taking the trouble to answer. He was a cocky and important figure among the *buscaderos*, and he knew it very well. Not even Lace Morrow could throw him off balance.

But there was more in the manner of these men than could be explained by any expectation of theirs that Tull Farris would object to another man paying too much attention to his favorite.

Another explanation occurred to Lace—that Bella had been set upon him, perhaps to draw from him the real reason for his visit to the Valley. That thought would have been Tulsa's. But Lace thought of no way now to settle it, even if it mattered. And with Bella going to Tull Farris to report what she had learned, the incident seemed unimportant.

Interruption came too, even if he had been inclined to go into the matter. Hoofs thudded outside, and there was the noise of a horse sliding to a stop. A man's voice lifted. Then Lucio Delgado appeared in the doorway. He blinked for a moment and Lace, watching him fixedly, suddenly grinned.

"Well, well, well! Look who's here," he cried. "The would-be poker player from Ancho!"

Delgado's face jerked that way and he glared at Lace. Then, with his short cat-like steps, he came toward him.

"Funny," Lace told the men at the bar, "I run into Delgado at Ancho and I never had a notion that he belonged in the Valley. I thought he was just some loud-mouthed cowboy from the Border and when you've seen one of them, you've seen 'em all—Heard 'em all, I reckon I might say. And here he turns up."

He grinned at the Mexican. "And where is our long and sad-faced friend, Topeka? Topeka—" he spoke again to Gano Brown and the others, while watching Delgado steadily "—is a man who never talks unless he's got reason. That's right, *no es verdad*?"

"I, Lucio Delgado, say to you—"

Lace lifted a hand—his left hand.

"Ah, now," he counseled, "don't go making any of those rash promises. You ought to know how they ended last time—in Ancho. Here I am, full of Tull Farris's whisky, and feeling right peaceful toward all the world. You wouldn't make me pick you up and throw you out into the street again? Don't say it! I'll take it as a favor if you don't. I just don't feel like getting worked up, right now."

Delgado's thin face was twisted. But after a minute he controlled it and spun upon one heel. He moved in to the bar and snarled at Ike.

"All right, all right!" the bartender told him calmly. "Don't you go yelling at me. You'll get your liquor and you'll pay for it. But you ain't big enough and you ain't bad enough to make us jump around here."

"My Lord! Another man Delgado can't make believe him!" Lace said very clearly.

Then, drawing upon a fairly active imagination, he told the story of the poker game in Ancho, of Topeka's "accidental" shot at him, of Delgado's attempt to kill him under cover of the table.

"And that fellow that was playing with us—" he was looking at Delgado's rigid side-face now "—if ever you meet him again, Delgado, you certainly ought to put the drinks out. For he saved you getting killed, that's exactly what he did! When he spread you over the floor he saved your life!"

Delgado ignored him. When he had finished his drink he walked across the room and vanished through the door into the back room, the one through which Bella had gone a few minutes before.

"So you run into Delgado in Ancho?" Gano Brown said slowly, seeming to choose his words carefully. "How come you didn't give'em the high sign?"

"Oh, they didn't look like anything special to me. The way they'd been hanging around, waiting for Dave Crews to show up, I thought they might be a couple of deputy sheriffs. That reminds me, how is old Dave these days?"

Gano Brown shrugged. His heavy face was

96

expressionless. "All right, I suppose. I ain't seen him for a long time. Same old liar he always was, last time I run into him, here at the bar. Why?"

"Why?" Lace repeated blankly. "Why—nothing! He was just one of the fixtures around here, and I wondered if he still hung out in the Valley. You been pretty busy, Gano?"

"Busy," Gano nodded sourly, "but not doing very much. I staked out a good job over West. We put a cottonwood down across the track and had all our work for nothing. They'd switched the money shipment we was after. Then Chick went down into Mexico and he run into half the *rurales* in the world. He got pretty well battered around before he made it back to the river. They chased him right up to the bank."

For a while they yarned of jobs and of men. Many of those whom Lace had known in other years—before the days of his ranching—were now gone. Some had been killed while attempting robberies, others had been arrested as far away as New York State, some had gone to South America to start life again.

While they talked, Lace was alert for any hostility that might show from front or back. From the back room where Delgado and Farris were probably sitting, or from the road outside, where Topeka Gates might appear. Topeka had tried twice in Ancho to kill him. The question which Lace asked himself now was whether he would carry that feud into the Valley here. He looked at Gano Brown.

"Who are those two—Delgado and Gates?" he demanded. "Supposed to be something special?"

"All I know is they was here when we come back. They don't belong to us—to Chick or me. They're working for Farris. So's Tom Elton."

"The reason I asked is," Lace told Gano Brown softly, "I've got a bone to pick with the both of 'em."

"Tull won't like bone-picking with them two," Brown assured him, and this time his tone was not unfriendly. "They do a great deal of riding around for Tull."

"I see," Lace nodded. And he was seeing—seeing Dave Crews' body lying in the road, after Delgado and Gates had met the nester.

Out of the back room, Tull Farris appeared suddenly. Behind him came Delgado and Topeka Gates. Tull led them straight up to the group at the bar.

"Lace," he said genially, "the boys told me they kind of got cockeyed on you in Ancho. They didn't have a notion that you was one of our kind belonged over here. In fact, they kind of figured you out for some kind of sheriff! And then you went to poking around in their saddle bags and naturally they figured you for a John Law. So they tried to rub out your mark."

Lace lifted one hard mouth corner in a small, contemptuous grin as he looked past Tull at the pair. "If either one of'em was fit to be left out by himself—even in a short-grass country," he said deliberately, "they'd have rubbed out my mark. They certainly had plenty of chance to—damn' sight more than most men ever get."

"Now, now," Tull said quickly, when Delgado bristled and Topeka's sullen eyes rolled ominously to Lace's face. "They're good boys. They work for me. I like 'em both and I like you, Lace. The thing is, the three of you have got to live close together while you're here in the Valley. You know we don't want trouble beween our own kind. The boys was mistook about you, same as you was about them. Now, there's not a bit of use carrying the fight no farther. You can see that plain enough.

"It wouldn't be a fight," Lace assured him, looking from face to face of the men behind Tull. "But if what you're getting at is, you don't want me to kill the two of 'em, I'll promise you that, this far. If they don't bother me, they'll live a sight longer. But, it does seem to me that things have kind of changed around the Valley."

He shook his head gloomily. "If it wasn't for finding Chick Haynes and Gano Brown and their boys here, I wouldn't know exactly what to think. These fellows that are drifting in nowadays, they strike me as being a pretty sorry lot!"

At the bar, Tulsa, Noisy and Dynamite stiffened. Lace looked directly at them—directly and critically. He shook his head again.

"Never mind all that, Lace," Tull told him sharply. "This is my Valley. You ought to know that by now. The right kind of *buscadero* can find anything he wants around Tull Farris' place. And there ain't much I ask a man to do. But one of the things is, he's not going to come in and start raising blazes with everybody else in the place."

"Now, there you go!" Lace interrupted him triumphantly. "That's what I'm talking about. In the old days, if a man said something in the Rock House, everybody there figured out whether he liked it or not. If he didn't, he did something about it. But you're after a promise, and you get it. Keep those two imitation gunfighters out from under my feet and they won't get stepped on. I'm doing this for you—because you seem to feel that they have got some value for you."

Tull Farris decided to leave it at that. He turned and ordered drinks for everybody. He stood beside Lace as they lifted their glasses.

"Who's that fat fellow Delgado was telling me

about?" he asked in a low voice. "The one that smacked Lucio when he was trying to get you."

Lace frowned artistically. "A pretty salty kind of saddletramp," he said reflectively. "The kind of fellow you know, without much thinking, that you'd like to have along to side you, in a tight. If I hadn't had so much on my mind, I think I'd have sort of inquired around about that man. He called himself Curly Camp. I was coming over to the Valley and I didn't feel exactly free to bring him over. Even if he was willing to come. I—*Amor de dios*! Why, there's the man himself!"

All eyes in the bar-room turned to the thick figure now halted in the doorway.

Curly Camp came waddling toward the bar with a wide grin upon his round and innocent face. Lace knew that Tull Farris was giving him one stare for every look turned upon the newcomer. So he frowned.

"It hardly seems possible!" he said—loud enough for Tull to overhear. "He got by the guard at Lookout, somehow—"

"Howdy," Curly Camp greeted them. "Who's Tull Farris?"

Tull moved out and stood regarding the fat, red-headed man watchfully. "My name's Camp," Curly informed him. "Up in the north I've gone by the name of Cole with the sign of Streaky Lightning. Maybe you've heard about that?"

"Curly Cole," Tull Farris repeated incredulously. "Of course I know who you are! But I never thought to see you down this way. Didn't they loop you and—"

As when Lace had put the same question, Curly nodded. He told briefly of his sentence to the penitentiary and of his pardon.

Lace was very much amused at the effect Curly

100

Camp's appearance had on Delgado. The little Mexican stood with snarling face behind Tull Farris—as if he could hardly hold himself from leaping at the easy, hulking figure which seemed all unconscious of his existence. Topeka Gates had better control of his features. He merely stood with dull eyes turned toward Curly, his lank body relaxed.

Then Curly turned abruptly and grinned at Delgado. But when he spoke it was to Tull Farris.

"This fellow tell you how I saved his life, over at Ancho?" he grunted. "Well, I certainly done exactly that!"

"I—heard something about it. Enough about it!" Tull admitted. "Why'n't you tell Lace who you was?"

Curly shrugged and for the first time looked directly at Lace. "I didn't know exactly about you, fella. I kind of wondered if you wasn't the Lace Morrow I'd heard about a time or two. But in this business you can't be too careful, and it seemed to me I heard something about you jumping off the high lines and setting up to be a first-class nester."

"They wouldn't let me nest," Lace told him with grim humor. "I've been on the dodge for a long while, this time. Well, anyhow, I'm glad you decided to drift over here to the Valley. Tull, here, is the chief schemer of all this neck of the woods, in case you didn't know. When he puts a hen on, it's a fat hen. He claims that if the boys always just follow his map they'll never come into trouble."

"That's right," Tull agreed calmly. "I've got all kinds of ways of getting the lowdown on things. So, when I scheme one, she's schemed."

"Your jobs have got too much killing in 'em, though," Curly said frowningly. "Take that Pluma job I

101

heard about. I suppose you schemed that one? Well, anyhow, it looked like a bunch of dang' foolishness to me—killing three altogether. Dropping the bank and express people during the robbery might've been something the bunch had to do, if the other fellows was shooting at them. But killing that fella that was just putting his head out of his door to look at 'em—That's bad and the kind of thing I've got no time for. That's not good scheming!"

Tull's face colored an angry red, but he had never been known to speak loosely, simply because he was irritated. "I didn't scheme that one, happens," he told Curly. "Lace and me was trying to figure, just today, who did pull that one. It wasn't anybody out of the Valley. That is, not so far as I know."

Gano Brown scowled at him, when Tull's eyes seemed to wander his way. "If you're looking at me, Tull," he began angrily, "when I do a job, I'll say I done the job. So—"

"I'm not accusing you!" Tull told him quickly. "Don't go off half-cocked!"

"I don't!" Gano assured him grimly. "But when I go off full-cocked, I hit something. About that Pluma job, looks to me like Barto Awe—"

"But Barto's up above Guadalupe," Lace put in smoothly, quickly, with a frown.

Tull shot an ugly glance at him, but Lace ignored it.

"Yeh," Gano agreed mockingly. "But when'd he go up there on that cow-steal? Two weeks ago!"

"Well, anyhow," Tull announced flatly, "'twasn't Barto on the Pluma job, so far's I know."

They let Pluma drop. The talk was general until Tull, with Delgado and Gates trailing, left the bar-room.

CHAPTER 15

LACE AND CURLY FOUND THEMSELVES ALONE IN THE center of the bar, after a while. Gano Brown and Tulsa's bunch had withdrawn to their original position near the front door, after some talk of the northern country and of *buscaderos* whom they all knew. Lace thought that his sitting here with Curly would now seem a natural thing. Everyone here understood that Curly had interfered on his behalf, against Delgado and Topeka Gates in Ancho.

Curly looked across the bar at the shelves on the back wall and spoke in a low voice, keeping his face blank.

"Well, I take it you never got a line on the Pluma job. Maybe I oughtn't to have mentioned it, but it did seem to me I had a kind of natural way of putting it, being an outsider but still an insider. Hope I didn't queer something—"

"Not a thing in the world!" Lace assured him. He spoke in the same guarded voice and with equal lack of expression. "No, if I could have ask' you beforehand to put it a certain way, I couldn't have wanted it put differently. You smoked up Tull and you sort of jerked out of Gano Brown what he would hardly have said to me."

"You don't stand too well in the Valley, seems to me," Curly suggested. "Farris was not a bit fond of you when you brought Barto Awe into the talk."

"No! He's suspicious of me, all right. And Gano believes the Pluma job was one of Barto's, the same as I do. He can recognize the earmarks of Barto's killing mania. And, of course, there's the knife Judge Bettencourt showed me, the one with Barto's road-sign on it, that was picked up on the edge of Pluma after the gang had hightailed. That by itself is not enough, but tied to the little things I've seen and noticed, it makes me pretty certain that Barto pulled the job."

"With Tull Farris furnishing the map," Curly nodded. "Before he hit for this Guadalupe place on the cow-steal."

"Yeh. The Guadalupe job is likely no more than a cover for Pluma. Tull's no fool! He knows well enough that this country is going to be hotter than a furnace for the men who downed Peters and Winst and that townsman. And another thing!"

He looked cautiously up and down the bar. Ike was serving drinks to the mixed crowds of Gano Brown and Tulsa Jack. From the half of the bar-room which Tull had partitioned off to serve as dance-hall could be heard the tinny jangle of a piano sadly out of tune. Someone was picking out *The Girl I Left Behind Me* and making hard work of it.

"I probably have told you enough about this Dave Crews hairpin to make you understand the part he played in Tull's schemes. Dave had been one of Tull's spies for a long time. And he was always hard to handle, always wanting a li'l' bit more than Tull had agreed to pay him. And he generally got it! Because Tull would need him for some other scouting and because Dave knew a lot about a lot of things. It's not going too far to say that every time Dave picked up a rope, the *buscaderos* here in the Valley got cold chills. They knew he could drop the loop around their necks and they wondered if he aimed to do exactly that thing!"

Ike came along the bar and stopped to grin at them. "You two have certainly got that swelled-up Mex's number," he said generally to them both. "I swear I

104

don't know how he's lasted as long as he has. Ever since he hit the Valley he's been asking for a couple of ounces of lead. But he certainly ain't taking chances with you two! Lucky for him . . ."

"Now, Ike!" Lace said reprovingly. "You know you heard me promise Tull I wouldn't nick the coupling pole for Delgado and Gates. And Curly here is off the same bolt. We're peaceable men, Ike. All we want to do is sit before the fire with our carpet slippers on, with a good bartender taking care of the liquor situation and old Concha out yonder to fling the frijoles at us. We wouldn't bother the like of Delgado and Gates."

"Yeh!" Ike scoffed, wise head upon one side. "And I reckon you'd do a li'l' knitting whilst you was setting before the fire, too, maybe."

"Tatting," Lace told him gravely. "Knitting, I hear, is a sheepherder game. Run into an English professor one time. He was collecting faces in the cow-country. He told me about the English sheepherders knitting while the sheep chewed up the face of Nature. Seems they wear shawls, too! Give us a full bottle, will you? It's really on Tulsa's gang . . ."

The bottle came and they drank sparingly. Very briefly, Lace told Curly of his encounter with Frio at the Rock and of the poker game at the cabin—and its flaming end. Curly nodded. But he attached no more importance to the incident than Lace had. He reverted to Dave Crews.

"Seems to me that a *gunie* like that would be carrying his neck sort of tender," he said. "Some fella'd figure it out that Crews wouldn't do much talking after he collected a .45 slug in his middle. I would, and I'm no big mind!"

"That's what I'm wondering about—in connection

105

with the Pluma business. Who was go-between, I've asked myself, when word of exactly when to hit and how to hit came to Tull? And I keep thinking about Dave Crews and how Tull sent Delgado and Gates to rub him out. There's one more thing that sort of interests me, here in the Valley . . ."

He shrugged and grinned a shade self-consciously. "Tull's got a kid here, a youngster that looks like some nester's girl. Nothing to make anybody go wild, skinny and all scared eyes. Delgado and Gates brought her in from somewhere about three weeks ago. Tull put her into a cabin by herself and made a sort of touch-me-not out of her. Bella—the queen of the Valley—is raising Cain because this Marian kid seems to be Tull's soft spot, and me—hell! If Tull ever had a soft place it was long and long before I ever met the gentleman."

"But—what're you driving at?" Curly demanded, frowning.

"Tonight I'm going to slide down and see if I can have a wawa with her. Maybe she knows something that'll clear up a little of the puzzle the Valley seems to have these days. I don't know. But I'm going to try. I—"

It had grown dusk outside the Rock House. Inside the bar-room the gloom was heavy; men seemed no more than shadows. Ike was moving to light a big oil lamp that hung in a bracket on the wall behind the bar. Mechanically Lace checked himself to watch—and to let Ike get out of earshot.

He was watching the bartender when the shot came. For once in his lifetime he found himself taken utterly by surprise. He had not expected any trouble here in the Valley, after Tull's lecture on deportment. So that shot, coming from around the door through which Tull had led Topeka and the Mexican, found him leaning easily on the bar, both arms upon its top.

Automatically, he turned—and was conscious of Curly moving beside him. Mechanically, he began to reach for the walnut-handled Colt that, since Ancho, had been sagging on his right thigh in a hand-carved holster. But the man shooting had corrected his aim. The first slug had fairly breathed upon Lace's cheek in passing. But the second struck him in the groin and doubled him instantly with the agony of it.

He came to his knees and drew his pistol. There was a dusky shape near that door into Tull Farris' quarters. He concentrated upon it, fighting off thought of the nauseating pain that came from his belly. He fired but heard a shot over him even as he let the hammer drop. He propped himself up with his left hand and gaspingly steadied himself.

The thought came that he had never known a man shot as he had been—in the groin or the stomach—who had recovered. Even with the best of medical attention a man with an abdominal wound died in agony. And here there was no medical attention to be had. But one thing he could do—he could see that Delgado or Gates died with him or before him.

But the man who had fired was not standing, now. He was a mere huddle on the floor in front of that door. And Curly Camp was walking past Lace, going toward the fallen man with his pistol ready. Lace saw everything—even to the tiny wisp of smoke that curled up from the muzzle of Curly's Colt. Then he fainted.

"Come out of it!" a voice was ordering him roughly, when next he heard anything. "You're all right, fella! Come out of it! Give us that whisky, Ike. A jolt's what he needs."

He moved, there on the floor, and opened his teeth to accept the neck of a bottle. The whisky ran into his mouth and with it the pain was lessened. He opened his eyes.

"What—happened?" he demanded, thickly.

"Delgado's intentions was blame good," Curly Camp told him. "Trouble was, he didn't know you packed a court house clock in your overalls pocket. His slug hit the watch and bounced off into the bar and we've been picking pieces of the old Waltham out of your belly for a half hour."

He sat straight and looked down at his groin. There was a great red blotch upon the skin.

"I'll be danged!" he said irritably. "Imagine going out over a poke in the stomach! What happened to Delgado? You get him, Curly? I saw him drop, saw you walking in at him—"

Curly shrugged. His round face seemed entirely unfit for expressing anything connected with murders or shooting affairs. Tull Farris spoke for him. It was the first time Lace had noticed Tull standing beyond the fat *buscadero*.

"Somebody got Lucio!" Tull said easily. "Curly shot twice and you shot once, and there's two holes in Lucio's heart you could drop a playing card over."

Lace began to scramble up. His bruise hurt, but he was no longer sick. He leaned on the bar and looked around at the faces of Gano Brown and Tulsa Jack and their men, at little Chick Haynes and three other men, finally, at Curly and Tull.

"I reckon Lucio figured he couldn't take the kind of talk you handed him," Tull said calmly. "I give him the powders not to start trouble with you, and I thought he *sabed* the burro. But he must've got to my bottle after I

108

left him and taken too much for his own good. Anyhow, he come out shooting and—you know the rest. I run in to try to stop it when I heard his first shot, but he was dead before I got here."

"And where's Topeka Gates?" Lace demanded grimly. "He was Delgado's li'l' playmate and he's got a habit of shooting into a lighted room out of the dark. He tried it on me in Ancho, and the more I think about it, the more I aim to break him of that habit. Now's as good a time as any, if not better."

He moved and screwed his face as the stab of pain caught him. Curly held out his dropped pistol silently. Lace took it and ejected the empty shell. While he reloaded, Tull Farris moved nearer him.

"Now, Lace, naturally you're sore—and nobody can blame you. But Topeka ain't going off half-cocked the way Lucio done. He ain't going to try drygulching you—"

"He better not!" Chick Haynes snarled. He was a bitterfaced little man, with only one eye. "First time he tries any bushwhacking against Lace or any of the rest of our crowd, we certainly will roll him up—what's left of him—and hang him high in a cottonwood. He's your pet, Tull; you better keep him under your thumb tight. You told Delgado what was what and look what he done. You better make certain Topeka *sabes*."

"Thanks, Chick," Lace told the little man. "Been ages since we held off the *rurales* outside Cananea, huh?"

"Five year, I reckon," Chick nodded. "Nice fight, that was. Glad to see you back, Lace. We tried to clear you with lawyers and money, but it took your own fist and guts to get you loose. Well, Tull? Figure you can handle Topeka?"

Tull nodded and went out of the bar-room. For a time Chick Haynes and Lace traded history. Then all the men

109

in the room went out to Tull's kitchen. Old Concha and two Mexican girls brought supper for them to a long pine table. Curly was well received by both the Haynes and the Brown men. Tulsa Jack and his men were quiet, talking only among themselves.

"Don't know if you was smart or not to come down here," Chick Haynes said at last to Curly. "We ain't doing so good, seems like. Gano run into a switched money shipment and me, I collected a lot of grief in Mexico, last time down for cows."

"Got some outsiders cutting the herd, looks like," Curly nodded. "Take that Pluma job that nobody knows about. Forty thousand in bills that just need signing . . . Maybe you fellas in the Valley ain't doing much, but somebody's doing good!"

"Outsiders!" Chick said frowningly. "What do you mean, outsiders? When I heard about that Pluma business, I said it was a Barto Awe job. Didn't you, Gano?"

Gano Brown nodded, but he was staring oddly at Curly. Lace saw Brown's expression and wondered if Brown were not thinking that this Pluma affair popped up very frequently. So he said thoughtfully that Barto Awe was up above Guadalupe, but Gano thought he might have done the Pluma robbery before going. And he shrugged at the end and made a cigarette.

"What difference does it make, anyway?" he dismissed the matter carelessly. "Somebody got all that nice new money. If it didn't come to the Valley, Tull Farris is the only one of this crowd to kick! He's the loser, not us."

And presently he got up, followed by Curly. They paid old Concha and went out. Lace leaned slightly to Curly.

"Going to be good and dark. Kind of keep an eye on things will you, while I sneak down to Marian's cabin?"

CHAPTER 16

THE CABIN WAS DARK. LACE HAD REACHED ITS WALL as silently as a big cat. He crouched in the moonless darkness beside it and listened. What he expected to hear he hardly knew. Certainly not the sound of any one following him. He knew of none in that Valley who could have trailed him as he moved up and back its length, before finally coming here.

He got up after a few moments and prowled around the four walls. As he passed a small, shuttered window, he leaned to put his ear close to it. Suddenly, as he listened, he felt an emotion which not even the sight of the pale girl cowering before Bella had roused.

There was something about that pitiful sobbing in the cabin which was childlike and touching. He rapped softly on the window. The crying stopped, ending in a stifled coughing fit. Silence followed. Again Lace rapped—more urgently. He heard the faintest sound of footsteps coming to the window. A thought came to him. He fished in a pocket and got out the gold locket which held the picture. He waited.

"Go away!" a low voice said shakily, but with some attempt at an imperative tone. "Go away, or I'll tell Tull Farris."

"I've got something to give you, Marian," Lace told her softly. "Something that belongs to you. And you needn't be worrying about me. I'm not one of the gang that's been bothering you. "I—he hesitated artfully— "maybe I daren't tell you who I am. Because if the gang

111

here found it out—"

"Well, what have you got of mine? Put it on the windowsill, if you want to return it to me. Then go away. I can get it."

"All right, I'm putting it there. You take a look at it, then think things over. If you decide you'll talk to me about—about what happened before you came to Lost Souls Valley, I'll come back to the window and ask you some questions. Maybe I can help you. And if I can, I certainly want to."

He set the locket on the log sill and stepped backward. He heard the casement creak softly open, then the slight gasp Marian made when she had identified the object. He waited, and wondered if her curiosity—all he had to work on so far—would be keen enough to keep that window open. He hoped so! And presently, after what seemed ages, she called softly.

"I hoped you would take a chance on me," he said quietly, coming up to the window. "I'm Lace Morrow, an old-timer here. But there's things in the Valley these days that I don't just understand. You see, I've been out a couple of years. I was homesteading until—not long ago."

"You—I've heard of you," she said, and shrank back, away from the window. "You—you're Lace Morrow, the killer!"

"Yeh? I didn't know that. I have killed some men— men who needed killing and who pushed me. Nobody calls me 'killer' to my face. I'm on the dodge, but not because of killings. But what I want to ask you is, who are you? How'd you get here?"

"And why should I tell you that? Why should I talk to you at all?"

"Don't know," Lace admitted. "Of course, I did bring

112

back that locket of yours, with your mother's picture in it. Seems to me that a man who'd take that kind of thing off a girl ought to've given the girl some notions . . :"

"Where did you get the locket, anyway? And who said it was taken off me?"

"I got it from a man who bought it off a girl who got it from the man who got it from you! Yeh, all that. I won it at blackjack—or, rather, in a card-deal. No matter how. But what do you mean by saying that you gave it to somebody? If I had only known that, I probably wouldn't have bothered to bring it to you. I'm funny that way. I don't like people that give away their mothers' pictures."

"I had good reason for whatever I did! And—and I'm glad to get it back—and I do thank you for bringing it. I think the world of that picture and locket."

"All right then," Lace said, softening. "Now, answer me. What are you doing in Lost Souls Valley? What's your name?"

"Do you know Dave Crews, the rancher on Animas Creek?"

"Of course," Lace admitted slowly. "Everybody around this neck of the woods knows Dave. I've known him for years. Why?"

"He's my uncle and he's disappeared. Or he had three weeks ago. I suppose he's still missing, because Tull told me that he had men hunting Uncle Dave and as soon as something was discovered he'd tell me. He said today that the men haven't found any trace of him so far."

Lace stiffened. It sounded exactly like Tull Farris! It might be just any length of time before word drifted to this girl that Dave Crews had been found murdered on the Ancho road. Meanwhile, Tull had her here—

113

"You say Dave disappeared three weeks ago?"

"Yes, just about then. He had been nervous. He was afraid of some of the men who used to stop there. I saw it, and Tull says Uncle Dave had deadly enemies in the country. Perhaps he just decided to hide for a time, after being threatened. But he may be dead! And all I can do is stay here—Tull says it's the only place I'm safe, under his eye. And it's awful here!"

"Awful enough," Lace agreed grimly. "This is one of the best known outlaw hangouts in the country. Certainly it's no place for a kid like you. But—suppose you begin at the first and tell me what happened, in the way of threats and so on."

"Well, I was living over at Denton with an aunt," she said slowly, and now shakiness seemed to have gone from her tone. "She died and I had only Uncle Dave to turn to. So I came out to live with him on the Animas Creek place. He was a peculiar man, but he was always very kind to me. He—You say you knew him well and—and you're an outlaw . . ."

"Takes an outlaw to really know a lot of people," Lace assured her. "Besides, I'm a special kind of outlaw. I quit riding the high lines, started me a ranch over beyond Pluma. But when some outfit stuck up the bank at Darien, the John Laws used me for a snubbing post. I drew twenty years, even though I never touched the job. I broke loose and—here I am."

"I see," she said, if a shade doubtfully. "Well, one odd thing about the ranch was the amount of company we had. The hardest sort of men were forever riding up—always very cautiously, too! And they would stay overnight, never sleeping in the house, not even eating under the roof. And another odd thing was the money . . . Uncle Dave always seemed to have plenty,

114

though it seemed impossible that he was making anything from that poor little place."

"Did you—ever say anything about it to Dave?"

"Yes, I did. He told me that he had some he'd made in the cattle business several years ago. He hoped to make some more before all his savings were gone."

"Know any of the men who used to ride up?"

"Some I heard called by name. The only really nice-looking man I ever saw there was Seth Ramsay. He's a clerk in the Pluma express office. He began to come out to the ranch about two months ago—to see me, Uncle Dave said. But they were always talking, off to themselves. Seth Ramsay came out six or seven times, in all. Once, when he heard me speak to Uncle Dave about the money, he laughed. Uncle Dave didn't like it."

"Not much wonder," Lace said drawlingly, with a jerk of his mouth corner. "Dave Crews has been—well, never mind that. This Seth Ramsay from the express office in Pluma, he visited you a good deal and then— Did he just stop coming for no reason at all? He didn't make love to you or anything like that, and have a row with you?"

"Oh, no! He was always very nice to me. Sometimes he'd bring me candy from town. But he always had a lot of talking to do with Uncle Dave, it seemed to me. He didn't make love to me at all. He—he treated me more as if I was about twelve instead of seventeen. The nights he came out—"

"Didn't he come out in the daytime at all?" Lace checked her quickly. "Always at night?"

"Why—yes, it was always at night. I suppose he had to work during the day. And he'd ride up to the corral behind the house and whistle. If nobody else was there, Uncle Dave would go down to the corral and bring him

115

in. We'd talk for a while, then I'd go to bed and they'd sit up till all hours, talking. And then the big quarrel came—just before I came here. That was three weeks ago, and almost a month after Seth Ramsay's last visit."

Lace cast back quickly, to arrange the dates he knew. He had been almost three weeks getting here to this window from San Francisco. And the Pluma robbery and murders were now about six weeks behind today. Seth Ramsay, a clerk in the express office at Pluma, had been a regular visitor to Dave Crews before the Pluma affair. Before, but not afterward . . . .

"What kind of quarrel was it? Who was there?" he prompted the girl. "It helps to know the names of the men who used to be around Dave's place."

"And it helps to talk to someone who—who's not making love," she told him hesitantly. "I had been in Ancho visiting a girl there. Nobody was at the house when I left, except Uncle Dave. But when the liveryman from Ancho drove me back, four or five men were there. They were talking about some kind of business with Uncle Dave, and he seemed to me—oh, he was nervous, but he was stubborn, too. He kept telling the big, dark, hook-nosed man—"

"Barto Awe!" Lace grunted, stiffening there at the window.

"Yes! Barto Awe. He told him that he wasn't going to give up his rights. They were arguing terribly, and it seemed to me that Uncle Dave was glad to have me there. For they were quieter after I came into the house. But I was afraid. Barto Awe scared me, and some of the others were almost as bad. Then Tull Farris came in with a Mexican named Delgado and a very tall man he called Topeka. Do you know them?"

"Yes, I know both of 'em. But what happened? When

116

did Dave disappear?"

"That day. Tull Farris had always been very nice to me. He is a rough man and when he talks to men he seems very hard. But he wasn't rough with me. I was glad to see him that day. For even Barto Awe and the others listened to him and the argument wasn't so bad. Uncle Dave finally said he'd bring some whisky he had buried down at the corral. He went out, bare-beaded, to get the jug. And that was the last time I saw him."

"He just kept on going," Lace said under-standingly. "Not much wonder, either, with that bunch around looking for his tail feathers! What happened after he was missed?"

"Oh, there was a terrible commotion! Barto Awe and some of his men went out to look for him. And while they were gone Tull told me that Barto Awe hated Uncle Dave and would kill him if he could. He said that he controlled Barto as much as possible, but he couldn't always handle him. He was afraid to leave me there on the ranch, alone. So he sent me here with Delgado and Topeka and told me never to say who I was. And I don't know what happened to Uncle Dave—"

She began to cry softly and Lace, knowing Barto Awe and Tull Farris and the kind of Long Rider who would side Barto, shook his head grimly.

It was not hard to picture that scene in Dave Crews' little house, when Dave held out for more than he had been promised of the Pluma spoils. Evidently, that had been a council over the Pluma job. It was easy to "see" that job, now.

Dave Crews had been the go-between. He had arranged with Seth Ramsay for the information the *buscaderos* needed. That was the part he had played for years in Tull Farris' plans.

But the Pluma job had been no ordinary affair. The murders connected with it had made it certain that the killer-robbers would be hounded by officers for years. Nerves were naturally tight. And when Dave Crews had chosen this time for insisting upon more than a fair cut, he had signed his death warrant.

Accumulated dislike for their spy, on the part of Barto Awe and Tull Farris, had come to a peak that day. Tull, Lace knew very well, had always called Dave Crews hoggish, a man who played the safe part but wanted more of the returns than those who had risked their lives in getting them.

"He knew they had the axe ready for him," Lace told himself. "And he began to see that they'd kill him even with the girl there. So he played his last stall. He went out to the corral and snatched him a horse and ran for it. Probably, he hid out in the hills until the other day. But Tull out-guessed him. Tull knew that Dave always used Ancho and would have to come in there to get money and help. So he put Delgado and Gates on the trail and, finally, they got him . . ."

"Do you think there's a chance of—of Uncle Dave still being alive?" Marian Crews asked him at last.

"Sorry, but I don't. Not a chance. Now, if I tell you a few things—some things you ought to know—will you believe that I'm a friend of yours, trying to help you and telling you the absolute truth? For if you tell anybody what I say to you, there will be gunsmoke in this Valley that will mean my finish. And mean that you won't have a person left to help you. First. Do you want to get out of here? Get back over to the kind of people you have always known?"

"Of course!" she said without hesitation. "I never would have come here, except that I was so scared about everything, and I didn't know which way to turn. I gave Delgado this locket. He promised to carry a note to the people in Ancho I'd been visiting. Of course I want to leave here. Bella—"

"She's pretty rough on you," he agreed. "And nothing to what she would be if she had a free hand. Girl, this is no place at all, at all, for you. Bella's an old stager. She can take care of herself just about anywhere she lands, an old entertainer out of the cheap honkatonks. She's crazy about Tull Farris and she knows he's getting soft about you. So—"

"Tull? Getting soft—on me?"

But the gasped question was checked almost instantly, and Lace, looking shrewdly up at the white oval of her face in the darkness, guessed that she was recalling things Tull had said or done, which had passed unnoticed at the moment, but now had a different color. Grimly, then, he asked her, "Is it any part of your ambition to be queen of the Valley in Bella's place? Tull Farris being the king, of course . . ."

"I was a fool to listen to him!" she cried. "I would have been better off out in the hills, afoot. I can see it now! He told me yesterday that Bella would be leaving soon. There was no reason for him to say that, except— Oh, I was a fool! I've been a fool ever since I came to Uncle Dave's. He—He's not honest, is he? Uncle Dave, I mean? And Tull Farris—?"

"Good!" Lace said curtly. "You're beginning to put two and two together and see the easy answers. So, maybe I'll be safe in telling you some news. I've known Tull Farris for ten or more years. Dave Crews almost as long. Tull is the Big Auger of all the Long Riders, the outlaws, in this big slice of country. Nothing goes on that he hasn't got a hand in. Only a few of us that he

119

can't run or bluff. Dave was his spy; he looked over banks and trains and the like and found out when they could be robbed. But Dave was a hog about money. And that killed him!"

"Then—then he's dead?"

"As Pontius Pilate! Tull Farris had Delgado and Topeka Gates kill him on the Ancho road the other night. He would have had Barto Awe kill him at the house, but Dave hightailed. Dave knew too much, and he was always arguing with Tull and the others about his split on the money from a robbery. How he lived so long, I swear I don't know. But he's dead now, I know it. And you're here, with Tull Farris thinking to make you queen of the Valley in Bella's place. Everything he's done has been for a reason, what Tull figured a good reason. So—"

"And you want me to trust you!" she said with quick harshness. "You—another of the same kind! A train-robber! A killer! You tell me that Tull Farris lied to me and you want me to believe that you're telling the truth. And I saw you with Bella!"

CHAPTER 17

LACE LAUGHED, THERE WAS SO MUCH OF IRRITATION IN her voice. He watched her stiffen, there in the window.

"I never was much of a lady-wrangler," he said humorously. "So I couldn't say why you ought to believe me or not believe me. I suppose I'm a kind of peculiar person. Most men that have gone through the things I've had to buck are queer in one way or another. But I know pretty well what I am and most men know it, too."

"You went out with Bella! And you're a noted Long Rider—I've heard men mention you as one of the most famous. They say you're the fastest gunman on the high lines. That means killer, doesn't it? And now, you come to me—"

"I can always go away, you know," he reminded her. "Go on and let you figure out your little problems by yourself the best way you know how to cipher. Look here. I don't know how to turn myself inside out to show a girl what kind of in'ards I own. Even if I wanted to do that. It's going to boil down to your trusting me or telling me you don't. But I'll tell you one thing—if you don't get out of Lost Souls Valley one way or another, and do it fast, Tull Farris or one of his kind is going to grab you so sudden it'll make your head swim. And when you're grabbed, you'll stay grabbed!"

Abruptly, he put his hands up and covered hers on the sill. He held her for a moment, then relaxed his grip.

"There! Your window's wide open. I had hold of you and you couldn't get away. You couldn't keep me from coming on inside. But I let you go and I'm stepping back. You can think of that when you're trying to make up your mind about trusting me."

"I—I have to trust you," she whispered, after a pause. "I have to trust somebody and at least you haven't tried to catch me, as the others would have. And—I'll be honest with you, Lace Morrow. I want to trust you. I—I suppose I've been trusting you without thinking about it, even when I was telling you I didn't. What can I do? What can we do?"

"I don't know yet. But I'll rig a scheme of some sort to get you out of this. And I'll come back here, this way, as soon as I can, to tell you what's on the map. It'll have to be done right away, too. Because—Shut your

121

window, quick! You haven't talked to me, you don't even know me. Remember that, if anybody—Tull or anybody else—asks. Somebody's coming. I've got to get away from here."

He patted her slim hands jerkily and slid away from the window. He heard it close softly. Then he went on down the wall of the cabin and squatted at the corner. Down the other wall a tall shape came toward him, barely visible in the moonless dark. Lace tensed as he stared, then relaxed. Tull Farris . . . Coming to tell Marian more of his smooth lies, doubtless.

"Who's that?" Tull snarled. And though he could not see, Lace knew very well that Tull was pointing a pistol at him. But his own arms were folded and over the left forearm the muzzle of a Colt was trained upon the other.

"I said who is it?" Tull told him savagely. "You better talk up real quick, or—"

Lace came easily to his feet and moved toward Tull. "Why, Mis-ter Farris!" he said, in the stilted and good-humored manner of a man rather gone with drink. "For an old man, you do stay out late. Maybe you need a new bed, softer. Or is it your conscience started hurting you after all these years? I tell you, Tull—"

"Lace? What the hell are you doing around here?"

"I never figured to see you exposing yourself to the bad night air, like this," Lace continued cheerfully. "But, I suppose you've got somewhere special you have to go . . . And so I won't stop you here, talking. Good night, Tull. Don't bother a bit about me. I'm thinking and I'm waiting. I'm a patient man, Tull. I can bide my time like a century plant—you know, that big cactus that brings out its pretty li'l' bloom once in a hundred years, then curls up its li'l' toeses and dies. Besides, the way you' been acting, I got nothing to do but wait and spend my money on your rotgut. You run along Tull, and leave me to do my waiting. I don't want company. That lovely lady of yours got oryide and went off and left me. So—"

"What're you doing here?" Tull demanded again, more harshly than before. "Talk up, Lace! This is my Valley, you know . . ."

"Put that cutter away before I have you chewing the front sight off it," Lace countered amusedly. "You wouldn't ever try to slap leather with Lace Morrow. Not when he has a gun out already . . . Well, if you have got to know, I'm doing ex-act-ly what I said—waiting. Just waiting. And I wouldn't keep you from whatever important business you're heading to attend to. Yeh—" his tone thickened slightly "—I'm all right. I've got plenty of time. She's got to come out of that cabin one time or another and, if I have to hunker right here till broad daylight, I'll meet up with her then. She's a nice looking kid, Tull. Not on Bella's style, of course. But there's something about her that kind of gets under my skin. So I'll wait."

"Now, you listen to me, Lace," Tull said viciously, earnestly. "I'm telling you to stay away from this cabin—now and all other times. You hear me? I don't know what you're up to, but you stay away from her, just the same. That kid's not for you. Not for anybody the like of you. You go on, now."

"That's your notion! She's not for me, huh? Just for Tull Farris, maybe? Well, you mustn't try to act the pig, Tull. It might make trouble for you. First off, I sort of liked Bella's looks. Thought I would give you a run for your money there. But she don't want to buy any part of me. Way she talks, she's more than half stuck on that bushwhacking, yellow-livered louse, Barto Awe. So I figure that anybody who'd touch Barto with a county loop is not my kind. And I'm going to look this kid over and if I like her looks as well as I expect to, we'll get acquainted."

"I tell you—flat—stay away from her. If you figure you can cut any ice with Bella, heave your twine and see what you loop. My notion is, you'll snatch air. I never heard of Lace Morrow playing the ladies! But this kid ain't for you. And you better believe me, Lace! You better believe me . . ."

"Hush!" Lace told him softly. Mechanically, Tull waited, leaning close to him in the darkness. "Ah," Lace said oracularly. "Got a notion. Maybe I'll marry this kid. And why not? What are you gawping at? Say, you don't think I'm drunk? I'll bet you that's what it is, you think I'm drunk. Well, I'm just as sober as you are. I am that! Fat chance I had, starting out with Bella. Speaking of hollow legs, I believe the gal still loves you, the way she kept emptying that bottle to your profit and my cost. Run along, Tull. Leave me to my waiting."

He thought that he would have handed over his last gold piece—and cheerfully—to know what was going on in that shrewd brain, behind the face so close to his own in the darkness. Tull Farris was not a man easily fooled. Few bragged of getting the better of him. And now Tull was oddly silent for a minute that seemed very long. Suddenly, he laughed.

"You're a wild-eyed hairpin, Lace. No use arguing with you, I can see that. Reckon there never was. Come along with me and we'll talk some business that'll interest you. 'Course you're not drunk. If you was, I wouldn't talk to you about the deal I've got in mind. Come on."

"Nah. I'll talk business tomorrow. Want to wait for

124

the kid tonight. Mustn't mix business and pleasure."

"Hell, you can see her tomorrow. We'll talk to her then. You're sober enough to augur out a deal with me."

He slipped an arm through Lace's and grunted when he put his hand on the Colt Lace held. "Put it away! You got no use for a naked gun here with me. Let's go."

Lace reholstered the pistol and let himself be moved forward beside the boss of the Valley. "Bella says you brought that kid in from somewhere back in the hills. What'll you take for whatever work was done in the bringing? I've got some money on me and if some of the boys come drifting in with more—specially Barto Awe that never could play cards—I'll have plenty more. I ain't so rusty at blackjack and I can do better at poker. What do you want?"

"Never mind the kid, now," Tull told him soothingly. "I've got some notions you wouldn't figure about her. I ain't selling out."

"All right, then! Play you for her. Any game or any stunt you pick. Play you—oh, three hundred against her. Fair?"

Impatience came into Tull Farris' voice. *"Por amor de dios*! Of all the one-idee'd cluckers, you are the dang'est I ever run into. Never mind talking about her now. Come on up to Rock House. I've got a fat hen to put on right soon. Been scheming it a good while. Didn't want to mention it to you before, because—Well, if you have really got plumb cured of your fool notion about quitting the high lines, there's plenty around the Valley for you."

Lace grunted. He was careful to speak in the same thickened voice he had used before; and to speak carelessly, like a man lifted by liquor above usual seriousness.

"Tarnation! What difference does it make what I think about quitting the high lines? Nobody in that Pluma court room believed I was a nester, when they had me up for the Darien job. Tell Roy Jacks I'm just a pore cowboy more to be pitied than censured, like the gal in the song. See what he says. What's on your mind that'll put *dinero* in my overalls?"

They went steadily—except when Lace remembered to stagger ever so slightly—toward the dark bulk of the Rock House. Tull led the way around a corner, toward the dark back rooms of the place. He was humming tonelessly to himself.

Inside the kitchen a dull glow came from Concha's cooking fire, now dying away. Tull stepped ahead and scratched a match. Lace was alert, but Tull only lighted a wall lamp in the back room adjoining the kitchen and beckoned Lace in.

There was a bottle on the table and Lace moved to it. Tull stared blankly at him while he uncorked it and lifted it.

"I would have thought you'd had about enough red-eye for one day," he drawled.

"I'm the only man in the world that can say when I've had enough," Lace informed him, lowering the bottle. "One thing you want to remember when dealing with me, Tull. It's not how much you drink that counts, it's how much you can handle."

"Reckon there's a lot to that," Tull admitted. "Set down."

Voices of men at the bar carried to them as a muffled murmur through the heavy, closed door. From the dance-hall the piano sounded and occasionally the shrill, distant laugh of a woman. Lace sat down so that his back was to the solid wall. Tull, preoccupied of face, twisted a chair about and straddled it. He frowned at Lace.

"You had me bothered for a while, Lace. Dang' if you never! We all know there ain't a better man on the high lines than you, when you really ride with us. But even if you are good as all that, you're just one man. And there could be a time when I'd say your room was a dang' sight better'n your company. I thought that when you rode up."

"If you feel that way about it, what're you driving at?" Lace demanded. "If I'm not wanted in the Valley—"

"Wait a minute! What I mean is this. You're just one man and Barto Awe is five-six men. And if you had come up just to reach for Barto's tail feathers account he rubbed out Bob Vardon, I would back Barto against you. Because he's worth more to me than you are. You want plain talk, so I'm giving it to you. Any way you want to take it, Barto's might' near as good a man as you are and in some special ways he's better!"

"That's either a dang' lie or too poor a guess for Tull Farris to make! Barto Awe never saw the day that he was as good a man as I am, any way you want to take it."

"Oh yes he is! There's no fool squeaming around about Barto. When he starts out to do something, he does it. And if somebody pops up that looks like getting in the way, Barto will down that man and think nothing about it. But you—I bet you never downed five men in your whole time and you're called a wiz' with the sixes!"

"Three in all," Lace said comfortably. "And every one of'em was a sidewinder and I was pushed into killing 'em. The last being that crazy feather duster

127

Tulsa Jack had with him, Frio. Barto's crazy on the subject of killing. He likes it! He kills a man when there's no sense to it, just to kill him. That is, if it's safe! Barto wouldn't take a chance with me, of course."

"Ne' mind that. Barto and me get along fine. I furnish the headwork and he handles the muscle. I tell him what the job is and he takes his boys and goes and does it. And I wouldn't let you or anybody else bust that open. But, you said you could do without his scalp. So I'm figuring we can all work together. On this deal I'm scheming, Barto won't figure. Like I told you, he's above Guadalupe. There's going to be considerable cattle to handle up there, inside a couple weeks. Right now, I'm aiming at old Heinie Schurzman at Crow Flat."

"That's no dang' good for a notion!" Lace grunted scornfully. "Why, that old store of Heinie's is a regular fort. He can beat off any bunch we can put up against him, Heinie can. He's got enough men, what with clerks and the boys from his freight corral, to just murder us."

"Usual, yeh. But this time not!" Tull said, grinning.

CHAPTER 18

LACE PICKED UP THE QUART AGAIN AND MADE A GOOD deal of noise while drinking very little. Tull reached for the bottle and Lace thought that his maneuver was duplicated in Tull's pretense of drinking.

"No, this is one time we can tap that old iron box of Heinie's," Tull said amusedly. "One of Heinie's clerks has throwed in with us. He's even got the combination to that big safe. We won't have to use the giant on it. Ought to be plenty in there, the day we land at Crow

128

Flat. You know how Heinie acts the banker for half the cow-outfits in that country. It'll be simple as a-b, ab. We'll be at Crow Flat with dark on the night I pick. This clerk, Jonas, he'll unlock a door for us. We'll raise the blazes of a rumpus off to one side that'll pull the boys away from the corral."

He grinned wolfishly. Lace watched him with drooping lids.

"Just a few of our boys will be enough to go into that unbarred door and open up the safe and empty her. Won't take over a few minutes, then the bunch'll be gone with the *dinero*. Jonas'll even steer Heinie's men off in a wrong direction, if they want to take out after our bunch."

"It certainly sounds good enough, way you tell it," Lace conceded. "You say Barto Awe won't work on this job at all . . ."

"Don't need him, now that bunch from Green River's here. Gano Brown and Chick Haynes, with Tom Elton and Topeka Gates, and you and this Curly, and Tulsa Jack's crowd—Any more and you'd be falling all over one another. What do you think of that Green River bunch, anyway?"

He discussed the Crow Flat robbery in minutest detail. All the while, Lace was engaged in the very unpleasant labor of trying to decide what he should do. This detective work was growing more and more irksome. He wanted only to land Barto Awe and the others concerned with the Pluma murders. But it began to seem that he must make a decision even more difficult than he had expected. He tried to think of a way out, of some excuse for not taking part in the robbery.

"Who's going to boss the job?" he demanded suddenly.

"Chick Haynes. Gano Brown's willing to work under Chick. No slip-ups when that little tarantula is rodding the spread. It'll go like clockwork over there at Crow Flat."

Lace felt that he could not object—not reasonably and naturally—to the leadership of that efficient, one-eyed veteran. So, merely to make talk, he said:

"Who's handled this Jonas, the clerk? Who made the arrangements with him?"

"I reckon I started it. I got hold of him at the Chink's in Ancho, one day. Sort of started the ball rolling. Since, I've met him three-four times out from Crow Flat. But it was one of Gano's boys fixed up the final touches with Jonas. Tomorrow, late, he'll be at the foot of the Dragoon Head on the Ancho trail, to say exactly what's what on the money."

"Yeh. And if the yellow comes up in his back, or if he's just been stalling you-all and telling Heinie Schurzman what he was doing, we're going to wish we was in hell with our backs broke, that's all! I certainly would like to have a look at this Jonas, and a talk with him, before I risk my one and only and precious neck on his play."

"You certainly do want everything your way!" Tull cried irritably. "How the devil you expect to see him—"

He broke off, to stare frowningly at Lace. Then he nodded. "All right! Even that can be handled, if you want to see him. You can satisfy your mind that he's really crooked enough to sell out Heinie Schurzman. All you have got to do is take a ride. That boy of Gano's was going to meet Jonas at the foot of the Dragoon tomorrow before sundown. If you want to make the last wawa with him, go do it. Fix up the whole show—any man that rode with Smoky Hills knows the ropes backwards. See Jonas and put the fear in him. I'll tell Gano you're going."

"And how'll we know each other?"

"You can't mistake him. He's a skinny little towhead. About twenty-five year old. Light blue eyes. But when you see him, just ask if you didn't know him in San'ton'. He'll say he wasn't in San'ton'; he works at Crow Flat. You ask him how's tricks over there. He'll say they're quiet—now. Like that. Quiet, then he stops and says—now. You wait in the brush out of sight until just before dark, then go up to the foot of Dragoon Head and he'll either be there or come along right away."

Lace nodded. He was considering every angle, but he kept his face no more than properly serious. "All right," he said. "I'll take a look at Mr. Jonas and find out what he's scheming. And I may point out a few little things that can happen to him, if he's not a nice boy. Now, I think I'll turn in."

But when he stood up, he grinned suddenly at Tull. "Don't forget, though, that when I come back, we're going to play for that kid. I'm promising you that!"

"We'll talk about that after this Crow Flat job. Maybe I can tell you something, then, that'll change your mind about her. Anyway, go on now and forget her for a while."

Lace went out into the bar-room and found Curly Camp with a pair of Gano Brown's men. He moved up to stand beside Curly and order a drink from Ike. Curly faced him blankly. The group of them drank at Lace's expense. Presently, Curly and Lace stood alone. Lace was thinking of Tull Farris. Tull was the one man among all the Long Riders here from whom he expected an equal battle any time wits must be matched.

"I'm mightily near the white-haired boy with Tull,"

he told Curly in an undertone. "Yes, sir! And the funny thing is, it's not fooling me a li'l' bit. He's one of those special liars—the kind that mix up a lot of truth in their lies so you can hardly tell one from another. He's stalling for time, so he can do something he's got in mind about me. Let's go turn in. There's an empty cabin down the line. We can talk there."

When they sprawled on their blankets in the little cabin, Lace told Curly all that he had learned from Marian, and of Tull's sudden appearance there.

"And it was right then that he broke down and admitted how good a man I am, and how valuable to him I can maybe be."

"I don't see a puzzle there," Curly grunted. "He's gone on that kid, that's plain. And you come along and tell him you want her and aim to have her. Maybe he hopes you'll get yourself wiped out at Crow Flat. And maybe you will—if the place is like you say. What do you see in it, more'n you say?"

"Nothing! I just feel. I've got the notion, Curly, that when I rode into the Valley the other day I bothered Tull. Just how, or how much will be Tull's secret. But something's on the fire beside this hen at Crow Flat. Something that I'd bother him on."

"I'll ride up to this Dragoon Head with you," Curly said abruptly. "Two men are generally better'n one on the trail."

"No . . . No, I think you'll be more good to the partnership right here, keeping an eye on things that happen. And if you get a line on Barto Awe—what he's really up to and when we can expect him back—that will be about all we could hope for. There's things moving in this Valley that don't show as more than just ripples on the surface."

"You're the doctor," Curly shrugged. "But I would a lot rather be riding along with you than just standing around the Rock House bar, listening to the boys tell 'em scary."

One reason occurred to Lace, that might of itself explain all of Tull Farris' manner toward him—the girl. As he fell asleep he pictured her as she had been, cowering before Bella, and then showing as no more than a pale shape in the cabin window.

"The poor kid!" he told himself pityingly. "She's too pretty and all around too nice to be made a football in this dang' Valley, by Tull Farris or anything like him. She's got better luck than that coming, if I have a say in the business. I'll just say head down to you, Tull Farris. And you had better believe me."

The men of Gano Brown and Chick Haynes and Tulsa Jack watched Lace as they sat eating in the Rock House kitchen next morning. They yarned of this and that, and when he put an occasional question he was answered courteously enough. But there was a narrow-lidded suspicion this morning, which had not been noticeable the day before. Curly Camp they treated without reserve as one of themselves.

Neither Gano Brown nor Chick Haynes had put in an appearance when Lace went out to saddle Plata. Nor did he see the two leaders when he rode around to the front of the Rock House and turned down the line of cabins.

Bella looked from a window at him. He grinned and waved and her mouth—not yet rouged for the morning—climbed sardonically at one corner. Then she returned his greeting with a jerk of the hand. He rode on and, coming to Marian Crews' cabin, slowed the big gray and whistled softly.

The window swung inward and Marian appeared. She

was even prettier than she had seemed the day before. As Lace slapped hand to hat rim she smiled, and it made her look years younger.

"Did you happen to hear any of my talk with Tull last night?" he asked her. "Well, Tull has decided to take me under his wing. And so I'm riding out on a little job for him."

"I heard! I—It was amazing. If I hadn't been talking to you just before, I would have believed that you were so drunk you could hardly stand. I—I heard everything."

"Not quite! There was more of the same on the way down to the Rock House. More stalling of mine, about playing Tull for you. But I do hope you heard enough of his talk to make you sure of the part you're supposed to play in the Valley?"

The pale face flamed and that, too, increased her attractiveness, Lace decided. And also it deepened that odd feeling he held for her—an instinct of protectiveness that he had never known for any human being before. She was so young, so soft. And here she must make a stand against human wolves, make it alone, unless he stepped out before her.

"I won't be away long," he said gravely. "But, no matter what happens, you remember that Lace Morrow is a great, big, hard fist on the end of your arm. You said it was your feeling that you ought to trust me. I don't know why, but it's my feeling that I ought to prove to you that your feeling is the right one to have."

He sat Plata with head a little on one side and regarded her smilingly. And without thinking of what he said—"You do trust me . . . But—do you do any more than that? Do you—like me? The way I've come to like you, Marian?"

"I do trust you. And—you're not a hard person to like, now that I see more of you. I'm grateful—"

"Shoo! Just watch your step and try not to worry. I'll be seeing you in a day or so. *Hasta la vista!*"

He turned, where the trail curved, for a last look along the Valley. The window still framed her slim figure. He lifted his hand, and he was smiling absently as he went on around the elbow of the narrow trail that led by secret ways out of Tull Farris' little kingdom.

It was a familiar ride to him. By two in the afternoon he was sitting in the brush within five hundred yards of that natural rock formation which wanderers had named, long ago, the Dragoon. He smoked and considered his various problems.

He could hardly refuse to ride on this robbery with the *buscaderos* of the Valley. Refusal would rouse quick and dangerous suspicion on the part of Gano Brown and Chick Haynes, as well as with Tull Farris.

Nor could he escape taking part in a crime by giving away the plan to the law. Not even to old Heinie Schurzman could he pass a warning that would result in death for those who would attack.

Spy he was—even if a spy of a particular sort. Unofficial officer, too. But as he had told Judge Bettencourt in the very beginning, there were well-marked limits to what he could do, would do, in that role.

Certainly, giving up such as Chick Haynes and Tom Elton to the law-men with whom he had ridden and beside whom he had fought more than once, men who had shared with him their last food and tobacco and water—that was something he would die before doing.

"I'll stick to my original agreement," he said aloud. "I promised to settle Barto Awe's hash, but only if Barto

135

was the man behind the Pluma job. That is all they're bargaining with me for—to clear Wes Kincaid and make the murderers pay off for the killings. That's all I'll do!"

It was something after four-thirty, by the sun, when he left his post in the brush and began to work toward the Dragoon Head. It towered above the trail, perhaps twenty feet in height, overlooking an almost sheer slope of a hundred feet. When he came to the trail he looked down mechanically and nodded when he saw no fresh hoofprints. Jonas, then, had not been here yet. He should be coming up the trail from Crow Flat, and could be seen easily for the last hundred yards.

Lace leaned negligently against the rock. At a slight sound on his left, behind him, he dropped a hand instinctively toward a pistol butt and began to turn.

"Don't you now, Lace!" Roy Jacks commanded grimly.

CHAPTER 19

SLOWLY, LACE LET HIS HAND FALL AWAY FROM THE pistol and waited stiffly. He knew Roy Jacks far too well to try beating the sheriff's full hand with a draw.

"That's the boy," Jacks told him. "Put that gunhand of yours up slow—and high. Figure you're reaching for a star—one of the high stars. Fi-ine! Now, use your left hand to unbuckle that belt. Just let her drop and step away. . ."

Lace nodded. His face was blank. There was nothing in his manner to show the rage that was beginning to boil in him. He jerked the strap-end of the shell belt free of the buckle and let the belt and holstered pistol drop to the trail. He walked slowly away from the Colt—three steps.

"Of course you're packing another gun under your shirt, in your waistband," Jacks drawled. "Go in after it. But, Lace, if you're entertaining notions, stop and think a minute. I'm a dang' good rifle-shot. I've got you covered. I don't want to stitch buttonholes in you, but if you make a wiggle, more'n just pulling that gun and letting her drop—"

Lace drew the second pistol and stooped to put it on the ground. Once more Roy Jacks' voice sounded grimly behind him. "That's good sense, Lace. Just take a couple more steps. Good! Put your hands down, now, behind you. And if it happens you're packing derringers or some other kind of hideout, take a good long think . . . And then don't do it!"

Lace obeyed without hesitation. For it would have been thirty-third degree suicide to try a break before that rocksteady gun trained upon his back. Handcuffs clicked about his wrists. Then he turned slowly, grinning at his captor.

"You know, Roy, it does look something like your turn, this evening. I never thought the time would come when I'd be dancing to your fiddling, but it only goes to show that a man never knows. No, sir! He gets up in the morning in the pride of his constitution, the way the Scripture says. And before it comes good dark, blame' if he don't stub his toe and fall down right in some sheriff's jail."

"It's going to be my turn from now on, Lace," the little sheriff said not unpleasantly. "I'm tol'able fed up on your breakaways. So we won't have any more of'em."

"Ah, don't say that, Roy," Lace mocked him. "You

137

know well enough you're wondering right now what kind of trick I'm going to pull out of the old hat. You can't keep me, and well you know it. I'm one of those what they call free souls. The idea of being caged up just fusses me till I rear back on my haunches and show my gums, and when I roar the walls fall down. Yes, sir! You know I'll curl my tail and start breaking down the timber. The thing that's really worrying you is mileage. You don't know how far I'll ride with you, so you can't tell how much you'll collect. Oh! How come you happened to be squatting up here, like an old hoot-owl on a barn rafter?"

"Luck," Roy Jacks said in a careless tone. "Just luck. You got your hawse back in the brush? I seen you come into the trail afoot. Wait a minute! Let's just look you over proper. It wouldn't look right, searching you in jail, and bringing out four-five more cutters . . ."

He shoved a pistol-muzzle into Lace's back and took a heavy stock knife and pair of .41 derringers—very pretty, very deadly, bone-handled guns—from him.

"Now," he said pleasantly, if with a shade of triumph, "we can see about the hawse. You'll be riding Plata, I suppose . . . I heard he was missing out of a certain pasture."

"Don't bother about coming along. At your age, Roy, you ought to be saving your strength. It won't take more than two-three minutes to get Plata."

"Don't mention it! I feel pretty spry today. And I've got more time than anything else. I'll go with you."

They went down to Plata and Roy led the gray horse back to the trail with Lace walking in front—by request. Then the chunky bay of the sheriff was recovered in the same fashion. Lace mounted with some difficulty while Roy Jacks watched.

"And now, Roy," Lace said courteously, with lift of towy brows, "whither away? If you haven't got any objections, I'll do the honors. Well as you know this country—or think you do—there's maybe a spot or two I can show you. Lovely places, Roy. Scenery that's something to tell your grandchildren about. Tell you— just put yourself in my hands and I'll guide you. I think education's a grand thing. It can't hurt a sheriff, even."

"You know what you can do, don't you?" the sheriff inquired with a tight grin. "If you don't, I'll tell you. You can go straight plumb to blazes! There's places around here I never have seen and don't expect to see. There's trails I wouldn't even ride alone—much less with a sudden old *buscadero* like Lace Morrow along. Uh-uh! Ancho is just plenty good for a pore old country sheriff like me. And, Lace . . . I do hope you won't make any sudden motions while you're riding ahead of me. This pistol is a hair trigger. We'll just scoop up your hardware and be hightailing it for Ancho."

It was twilight when Lace's pistols were in the sheriff's saddle bags and they rode down the slope toward Ancho. Before they had gone a mile, Roy Jacks shifted in the saddle and with a dry whirring sound the loop of his lariat came through the air and noosed Lace. So they went on, coupled together, through the thickening dark.

All of Lace's deft questions went unanswered or received evasive replies. And at the last he made his definite decision—the same decision that had flashed to him with the sound of Roy Jacks behind him at Dragoon Head. Tull Farris had put the cross on him, had committed the unpardonable sin of the Long Riders. He had betrayed a *buscadero* in good standing to the Law.

There was no traitorous clerk at Heinie Schurzman's

store. There was no Crow Flat robbery planned. Tull had simply led him cleverly on until he himself had suggested coming to Dragoon Head to see this "Jonas."

And it had been arranged with typical Farris cleverness. Tull had not said a word to suggest his coming here into Roy Jacks' hands. He had simply pushed Lace into virtually demanding the right to see the crooked clerk and satisfying his own mind about Jonas' sincerity.

"*Amor de dios*!" Lace said wonderingly to himself. "He certainly did want me out of the way, to take this chance . I'm not altogether sure about Gano Brown and I'm too dang' sure about Tulsa Jack. But if Chick Haynes or Tom Elton or Curly Camp—happened to find out about this business of Tull sending me up to Dragoon Head after he'd arranged for Roy Jacks to be waiting for me, blazes would be popping right now— and right on top of Tull Farris' neck. For naturally Chick and the others would figure that if he'd toll me into a trap, he'd do as much for them whenever it looked good for him; that he'd put the cross on anybody."

He wondered if it had been finding him at Marian Crews' cabin which had suddenly hardened Tull Farris' determination to be rid of him. Lace shook a slow head. He admitted that he had begun to like the girl himself, like her very much indeed—more than he had ever liked anything in skirts. He would do a great deal for her. But Tull, it seemed, would do more! Apparently, he would commit almost any crime since he had committed the very blackest—in order to keep her for himself.

Lace grinned pleasantly and began to whistle softly, so that Roy Jacks asked what all the happiness might be about. Lace did not tell him that he had just made up his

140

mind to get away, escape quickly, and that he had just added Tull Farris' name to that list which held the Pluma robber-killers.

Instead of explaining, he began to gossip cheerfully concerning Roy Jacks' experience in San Francisco. It was proof of the sheriff s certainty that he now held the whiphand, that he would discuss freely and without rancor his captivity in Golden Gate Park. A policeman had discovered him handcuffed to the tree, after four uncomfortable hours in the chill breeze from the Pacific Ocean.

Lace nodded inwardly. Roy's willingness to talk of that uncomfortable and humiliating experience seemed to him something like proof that the sheriff had waited beside Dragoon Head because of information supplied by Tull Farris. Someone—Topeka Gates at a guess— had ridden fast out of the Valley the night before, as soon as it was sure that Lace Morrow would step into the trap set for him.

Jacks asked how Lace had made his escape from the surrounded rooming house on the waterfront and Lace shrugged. "You could hear those bluecoats walk a half mile away. Now, if they had brought you along, Roy, it might have been different. I just happened to hear'em up on Market Street. I said to myself, now, they certainly wouldn't be herding that bunch of buffalo out of Golden Gate Park, not down through the Main Stem of town. So I knew it must be the police."

"You kind of spattered O'Connor and some detective over the street, when you stepped out of that house," Roy Jacks remarked, not too reproachfully. "They caught the devil from their bosses when they come to and made their reports."

"Well, yonder's Ancho," Lace said thoughtfully.

"Wonder if they've got a bed for us down there, Roy? I didn't use the hotel there, last time in the town. But one time I was there, and the hotel was all crowded up."

"At the hotel we're heading for," Roy assured him dryly, "they would make room for us, whatever. Ancho has a small jail, and I hope you'll try to put up with our country ways, Lace, while you're with us. We'll do the best we can for you until you're down at Huntsville where they've got more room."

"I hope you don't mind my saying that I'm not planning to go to Huntsville?" Lace asked him politely. "A man can't be too careful about the people he associates with, Roy. I know I've been kind of careless one time or another, I've even had a lot of dealings with lawyers and sheriffs. But I just can't go for the kind of men I might run into, down at Huntsville. So, hoping you're the same, I'll not be with you long. How about going to an eating house for a meal? I've got money and I'm not reforming my ways this minute. I'll eat with a sheriff—hungry as I am tonight."

"You will like blazes! Not in a town outside my county. We'll head right for the jail and then you can send out for anything you want. Not for me any mixing a prisoner as slippery as you in a restaurant crowd. Uh-uh!"

He directed their course so that a circuit was made of the county seat. They halted before a long, one-story building of quarried stone. A light showed in the front end. Roy grunted to his prisoner, "This is the sheriff's office and the jail's behind it. Slide off the best way you can, Lace. And, once more, don't you start entertaining notions. That Frisco business was absolutely the last of its kind. I'm on my own heath now, like old *Rob Roy* in the story. You better remember it."

142

"You know, Roy, you mustn't get too cocky," Lace told him, lying flat upon Plata's neck and working his right leg up. "Nothing makes a sheriff more unpopular than crowing. And you want to remember, too, that about as many good riders have been piled by a bucker's last jump as ever come off at first."

He slid to the ground and worked his body until the loop of the sheriff's lariat dropped to his feet and he could step out of it. A man appeared in the door of the sheriff's office.

"What's all this?" he demanded. "Who're you men?"

"Sheriff Jacks, from Pluma," Roy answered. "Got a prisoner, and I'll appreciate your lodging him for the night, even if he has to double up with one of your own home-towners. Can do?"

"Sure, bring him in. Glad to do Pluma County a favor."

Lace moved toward the door and the jailer—a young deputy sheriff very fancy in red silk shirt and pearl-handled Colt, wide white Stetson and alligator hide boots—stepped back to let him enter. Carelessly, he looked at Lace.

"Glad to see you, Sheriff," he said respectfully. "Boss is down town somewheres—"

"Probably down at the Acme," Lace amplified that. "I played poker with him and some other outlaws, last time I was here. He's a young fellow that likes his bottle and he's gaudier, even, than our young friend here. Goes for spotted vests and all the dude-puncher regalia."

"Listen, you!" the deputy snarled, leaning forward. "You can easy get your dang' head cracked wide open. Who do you think you are, anyhow? You—"

"Name's Smith. John Quinn Smith. Crayon portraits are my business. But the sheriff, here, he has made a

143

terrible mistake. He thinks I'm Lace Morrow, some kind of *buscadero*."

The young deputy's mouth sagged as he stared from Roy Jacks to Lace. In a thick voice he repeated, "Lace—Morrow!"

Lace made a gesture with his manacled hands and Jacks handed the deputy his handcuff keys. "Uncuff him, will you son? I like to be out of arm's length of the wildcat. Yeh, that's Lace Morrow, the bank robber you've likely heard plenty about. And probably you ain't heard the half of what could be told. I want him stuck in the best cell you can furnish. Couple of my deputies'll be over in the morning and we'll herd him over to Pluma."

Still with awed expression, the deputy unlocked the cuffs and Lace worked his stiffened arms luxuriously, then fumbled in a pocket for tobacco and papers and made a cigarette.

"We'll go over him careful, too," Roy Jacks said to the deputy. "I wouldn't put it past him to hide something that'd deceive an officer—a set of jail keys or something like that."

He watched while the Ancho officer searched Lace carefully. But his money was all that remained to Lace and when that was locked in a cupboard of the office, Lace looked inquiringly at the sheriff. "And now how about letting this young fellow take some of my money to go buy us supper? And a quart of right good Acme whisky wouldn't go amiss."

"All right," Roy Jacks agreed. "Son, when you go down, you might tell the sheriff I'm here and I'd like to see him. But—don't tell him what for, and don't say a word about us having Lace Morrow in jail. No use taking chances on this hairpin having friends in town

144

that might make a try at letting him out of this."

The deputy nodded and went out. Roy Jacks settled himself comfortably in a chair near the locked door of the office. Lace hunkered on the floor against a wall and smoked. Suddenly, he pictured the sheriff's face as it would have looked, if he had been carrying that parole offered by Judge Bettencourt. He could see Roy Jacks drawing the folded paper from his pocket, opening it and reading with wide eyes and open mouth. He began to laugh and stretched out upon the floor to laugh more comfortably. Jacks eyed him suspiciously.

"Nothing to tell, now," Lace gasped. "You'll know, one day."

CHAPTER 20

THE SHERIFF CAME BACK WITH HIS DEPUTY AND THE waiter who bore meals for Roy Jacks and Lace. He was sober, tonight, and did not recall Lace from his other visit. He shook hands with Roy Jacks and looked curiously at the prisoner.

"We've got a good jail," he said. "All stone and steel bars. Cell block opens on a passage that's got just that one solid door yonder. The jail's empty, so you can take your choice of cells. Lock him in one, then lock that door. He won't get out of my calaboose!"

Roy Jacks chose the last cell of the tier, a steel cage set in a corner of the stone walls. Lace ate his supper locked in that cell with the officers in the passage outside.

"I'll just keep an eye on that cutlery," Roy told the Ancho sheriff. "I don't know what he could do with a spoon or a fork, but I just as soon he never had any."

When the three of them had gone back to the sheriff's office, taking Lace's tray and leaving a wall lamp burning in the passage, Lace sat for some time, smoking thoughtfully. A glance around had informed him that, for him, the only feasible way out of Ancho County's official hostelry was by the door. And with three guards on the road to Pluma, there would be little or no chance of escape tomorrow. Once in the Pluma jail—a stronger building than this—he would be hopelessly a prisoner. He shook his head scowlingly.

"And even if Judge Bettencourt was willing to come out with the parole," he thought moodily, "it would mean the end of trying to do anything for Marian Crews, the finish of my work on Barto Awe—and maybe my finish all around. Nothing would make Chick Haynes and Gano Brown believe that I was just after Barto's tail feathers, that I wouldn't have turned them in to the Law for any money. Somebody would always be looking for a chance to hand me what somebody ought to hand Tull Farris for his cross . . ."

He stared out through the door bars. There was a broom leaning against the opposite wall. He got up, face intent, and tried in every conceivable position to reach the broom. But it was too far away. He looked, then, at the litter of burned matches, cigarette stubs, old newspapers, muslin tobacco sacks on his cell floor. A mirthless grin lifted the corners of his thin mouth.

He yelled for Roy Jacks. Presently the door into the sheriff's office opened and Roy looked down the passage. He asked what was wanted.

"If it's more of the whisky," he finished humorously, "you are just bodaciously out of luck. You killed a pint and we finished the other pint."

"I want that broom. This cell's not fit for a pig to

146

sleep in. Le' me have the broom till I clean it out. I swear, even you are a better housekeeper than these Ancho people."

"Blazes, it's just for one night. Ne' mind trying to clean things up around here now."

"You gi' me that broom or nobody in this end of Ancho County will get any sleep tonight, I promise you that! Time I pound on these bars a while with a belt buckle—"

"All right! All right!" Roy Jacks surrendered. "I'll let you have the dang' broom."

He came grumbling along the passage and handed Lace the broom. Lace made so much dust that the sheriff retreated to the office, coughing. Thereafter, Lace merely kicked the litter with his feet while he worked at the wire lashing of the broom. When he had unwound as much of the wire as he wanted, he finished cleaning the cell and yelled again for Roy Jacks.

Roy came down the passage once more. He took the broom and set it against the wall. Lace, leaning against the door, said in a low voice, "Roy, I'm beginning to think that I'm one dang' fool and you're the other . . ."

The sheriff turned, a yard from the door. He stared curiously, yet suspiciously, at his prisoner. Lace shook his head frowningly and seemed not to look at him.

"And how am I a dang' fool?" Roy Jacks demanded.

"You want the gang that pulled the murders in Pluma, don't you? Folks are beginning to sort of rawhide you and you come up for election too soon for that to blow over. And what people are saying after only a couple of months is nothing at all, at all, to what they'll be saying when a year goes by and still you haven't looped that gang. Just you wait!"

"Maybe a year won't go by without my looping 'em.

147

What, exactly, are you driving at?"

He watched Lace narrow-eyed. Lace shrugged. "Maybe not. Of course, I can't say you're not right on their heels. But I have been places, lately, where talk of that kind of thing was likely to pop up. I don't think you own an idea in the world to work on. I don't think you can loop that bunch on your lone, if you live to be a thousand."

"Even if you know, you wouldn't tell me!" Roy Jacks said positively. "I know you too well to expect it."

"It's a queer thing," Lace drawled meditatively. "I've never crossed a man, yet. But that kind of murder is the kind I have got no patience with. Roy, who would you rather have, if you could have just me or just the Pluma killers?"

"The Pluma killers, of course! But—"

"Tomorrow we'll be riding over a lonely road. If you'll promise to let me make one of my famous breaks, I'll trust you with a li'l' secret about the men who killed Winst and the others. Blazes, Roy! Nobody expects you to hold onto me after you happen to catch me. You turn up with the usual tale—"

Roy Jacks swore angrily and whirled on his heel. And Lace thrust his hand out through the bars. The noose in the thin broom wire flicked up and dropped neatly over Roy Jacks' head, and settled about his neck. Lace twitched it taut and drew steadily upon the wire.

Roy Jacks was pulled remorselessly toward the door and his hands went automatically up to claw at the garroting wire. He had made no sound except a single harsh grunt. Lace caught his shoulder with left hand and held him moveless. The wire was buried in Roy's neck. His tongue came out and his eyes were bulging.

Lace jerked the Colt from the sheriff's holster, got the

cell key from Jacks' pocket. He let the sagging figure down and reached out to jam the key into the lock. A turn and a push and he was outside. There was no alarm from the front where sheriff and deputy waited. He dragged Roy Jacks into the cell and freed him of the choking loop, locked him in and went softly up the passage.

Sheriff and deputy were sitting at a table, on which was the empty quart bottle. Mechanically, they looked up at the doorway when the hinges creaked. Both stiffened at the sight of the pistol-muzzle trained upon them.

"Hi!" Lace said cheerfully. "Thought I'd come up and wawa with you a while. But, on second thought, you two had better come back with me. Roy Jacks is waiting for you down the passage. Up you come, young'n's! And reach for your ears before you move anything else. Kind-hearted as I probably am, shooting a strange gun this way I'd probably get you in the nose when I was just reaching for an ear."

Two pairs of hands came up as if the men had been punched. Slowly, they stood, faces masks of fear. Understanding, Lace grinned reassuringly.

"I'm not going to kill you! And Roy ,Jacks is just locked into a cell. Same for you two, if you don't force my play. Over against the wall there, and face it. Now—"

He disarmed them and searched their pockets quickly and expertly. Obediently they went down the passage before him, and Roy Jacks, sitting against the wall rubbing the thin, red weal about his neck, blinked furiously at Lace.

"Company, Roy," Lace told him grinning. "What did I say about you not being able to hold me? But you have got to admit one thing, same as I do. Our li'l' wars have always been carried on fair and above-board. If I ever do feel like being captured, I'll give you my business. In you go, you two! And you can remember one thing, all of you. I'm not going to ram gags into your mouths and tie you up. But I'll be around the place for a half-hour or so. You had better keep quiet for at least that long, or I'll come back in and really leave you in shape that'll make laughing stocks out of you."

His belongings were all in the cupboard where Roy Jacks had locked them. Plata was in the corral behind the jail. In less than three minutes the big gray was leaving Ancho, going fast toward Pluma. For, during the day, Lace had been doing some piecing together of puzzle parts. He had developed a strong desire to interview Seth Ramsay, the express office clerk who had made several mysterious calls upon Dave Crews.

It was almost midnight when he left Ancho. The twenty miles to Pluma were covered easily by four o'clock. Knowing the seat of Pluma County intimately, Lace came quietly between the walls of the Pluma Store and the express office just before dawn and swung down from Plata.

Already lights were springing up in windows, in this early-rising town. From the freight corral down at the end of the street the crack of a whip carried to him, then a freighter's harsh, angry voice, addressing some stubborn mule. A man came across the street toward Lace. He was whistling cheerfully and, when he was close, Lace identified him as the owner of a little eating house adjoining the Pluma Store.

"Looking for breakfast?" the restaurant man called pleasantly. "Have a fire going in two minutes and coffee on in fifteen. You're an early bird, fella!"

"Yeh. Drifting through," Lace told him huskily. "Lost

my road last night and slept out. Heading for Ancho. What time does the express office open?"

"Any time now. Seth Ramsay'll be along in a minute. We open up about the same time, but the difference is Seth can get back to sleep after he's checked his stuff for the first stage. Me, I got to keep going all day. Yon' comes Seth now."

"Fine! Got a package I want to send off. Busted a spur and it's guaranteed. Going to make the store stand behind the promise, too! Well, thanks! Be in after a while."

He watched the slight, quick-walking figure coming across the street. The light was gray, now. He could see the neatness which had impressed Marian Crews, observing Seth Ramsay in contrast to the roughly-dressed men who would usually make Dave Crews' place their stop.

The clerk stepped up on the wooden veranda and looked sharply at Lace. He had a bunch of keys in his hand. They jingled as he went toward the door. Lace did not shift position, where he leaned against one of the veranda posts. He said "Tull Farris, Ramsay. Ever hear the name?"

The words were like an explosion. Ramsay whirled clear around and the keys jingled on the veranda. He made a gasping sound as he cowered against the wall. Lace straightened and came loafing over to stand a yard from the shaking man.

"Why, you yellow rat," he drawled. "How Tull ever figured he could trust a thing like you, is more'n I see. Stand up! Nobody's going to hurt you—now!"

"Who're you?" Ramsay whispered stickily. "Who're you? I—I never heard of Tull Farris! I—I don't know what you're talking about! I—Who're you, I said?"

151

"Ne' mind. We've got some talking to do. Maybe you don't know Tull Farris, but he certainly knows you. And he's a li'l' bit worried about you, Ramsay. How's it been around here? Anybody been snooping around trying to find out about—"

"For God's sake! Don't say it! Don't mention that—that business! Roy Jacks—the sheriff, you know—he's been here a half dozen times. But he don't suspicion anything. I know he don't. For they're still holding Wes Kincaid in jail. And they wouldn't do that if Roy Jacks had suspicions. Nobody else has been around since the detectives made their first examination of the office and the bank and all. What does Tull want? Who're you? How do I know that—that you're all right?"

He was utterly frightened. Lace shook his head contemptuously and looked to right and left, to see that no other early risers were closing in upon them.

"You're a yellow rat just like I said! Not enough guts to hold horses for a Long Rider bunch. Ne' mind who I am! It's just plenty for you to know that I'm straight from the Valley. As for my being all right—of course you don't know that. You just have to hope I am! But I'd hardly know all the ins and outs of this Pluma job, if I wasn't all right. I know you tipped Dave Crews to the right time on the money shipment. And you got your split, same as he got his. I suppose you know who did the actual stick-up?"

"No! No, and I don't want to. Somebody killed Crews on the Ancho road and I went over to see him. I—I looked at him, and I wished I never had thought of listening to his talk of the money we could make. I could see myself lying on the road just the way he was—because he knew too much—"

He groaned, but Lace snarled at him.

"I—I suppose you're all right," Ramsay went on desperately. "You wouldn't know all this if Tull hadn't told you. But they promised faithfully that nobody would ever know about—about me, except the two of them. Crews and Farris. It's not fair for them to go spreading that around, telling you and everybody. If the company guessed. If Roy Jacks even had an inkling. I'm not cut out for this kind of thing. I wouldn't go through two months of it again for a thousand times a thousand dollars! I haven't had an easy minute since it happened. I wake at night in a cold sweat, dreaming that Roy Jacks is putting the handcuffs on me. And I haven't even got a chance to spend the thousand. If I went off and spent it somebody might guess where I got it and come down on me! I can't stand it—"

"Oh, yeh! I reckon you can. And you will. There's no better place for lightning to strike than right on the button it socked before. That's our motto. So, you look around for another nice li'l' package we can take care of. Oh! Karl Peters was a kind of good friend of yours, wasn't he?"

"In a way, he was. And that's another thing—I see his dead face night and day. But I didn't have any idea they'd kill him! I wasn't responsible for that. It was Karl's own foolishness. He didn't have to fight. He could have let Rod Stafford shoot it out, if Rod wanted to be a dang' fool!"

"Of course," Lace said calmly. "But what I want to know is, are you with us or—against us? I just want to know what to tell Tull Farris. Dave Crews, now, maybe he guessed wrong. You wouldn't want to guess wrong?"

"What can I do?" the unhappy clerk cried desperately. "I can't buck Tull. I'll watch for another money shipment. And—and this time, if I have to go through

153

all the agony, I ought to have a bigger share. I lay all the foundation, so I'm entitled to a big cut."

"Oh, don't you worry about that!" Lace reassured him solemnly. "You'll find that you'll get everything that's coming to you. I've got something to say about this business, now. I'll see that you get plenty or bust a hamstring. Yes, sir!"

He asked Ramsay for a piece of paper and a pencil. The clerk unlocked the office and brought out a shipment blank.

Lace thanked him and with the blank against the office wall wrote deliberately.

> Seth Ramsay at the express office is your
> man. But rope him right away. He tipped
> Dave Crews to the money-shipment and
> Dave passed the word to the gang that
> did the robbery and killing. Ramsay will
> squeal like a rat if you handle him right.
> You might tell him the penitentiary is
> the only place he will be safe. He says he
> was not told what gang did the job and
> maybe not. But what he will confess will
> certainly clear Wes Kincaid and that is half
> my job done. I will see you later. Ask Roy
> if the Ancho hotel has got good beds. But
> stand a little back from him when you ask
> how he slept.

He nodded to Ramsay and gave back the pencil. He told the clerk that he would be seeing him and grinned faintly at the sight of Ramsay's lessened fear.

The note was in his shirt pocket when he mounted and rode through the narrow space between buildings.

He jogged along the backs of Pluma buildings until he saw Judge Bettencourt's square white house in its half acre of yard behind a wall. A Mexican was moving about the servants' quarters when Lace rode quietly up to the back gate. He came at Lace's call.

"Here is a *carta* for your *patron*," Lace told him. "It concerns a certain horse in which the judge is interested. You will take it directly to him and say that he who brought it could not stop."

"But will it not be better for you to see the judge?"

"I'll see him a lot—I hope—but later on. Now, there are still horses to be located and corraled."

He touched Plata with a rowel and the gray moved on as if the miles from Dragoon Head to Ancho, from Ancho here, did not lie behind him. Lace looked down affectionately at him.

"You old cross between Original Sin and the *caballo* that was first off the ark! Get going! We're headed back for the Valley. *Seguro*! We have got to tell Tull what happened . . . We waited and we waited, patient as an old maid looking for a husband. But that deceiving Jonas clerk, he just never showed up at all, at all. Funny—and kind of sad, too! We're grieving about it, Plata. But think how Tull will feel!"

His shoulders shook, but hardly with grief, as Plata carried him away from Bettencourt's house. And presently he forgot the things which amused him—like Roy Jacks' language if anyone should inquire about his capture of Lace Morrow. There were too many things to consider as they moved toward the hills.

At a line camp he ate with a cross-eyed cowboy who knew him, but politely treated him as a stranger. Then he rode on into the beginning of a bright, cool day, and cut into the Ancho-Pluma trail again.

CHAPTER 21

THERE WAS MORE THAN ONE TRAIL INTO GUARDED
Lost Souls Valley. But few—very few—knew more
besides that which led past Lookout Rock and the sentry
always stationed there. But Old Smoky of Lace's
earliest outlawry had known the Valley even before Tull
Farris had moved in and built the Rock House and,
slowly and surely, had become tallest man of all the
buscaderos by virtue of his crooked, cunning brain.

And Smoky Hills had shown Lace everything he
knew of the Valley, as he had taught him gunplay and
trailing. So every narrow ledge and stock-track was
mapped in Lace's brain, as it lay in relation to every
other trail—and particularly to the Main Drag which,
mounting mesa and ridge very often, overlooked most
of these weblike ways of the Long Riders.

He made the Drag in mid-morning, and it would have
been a sharp-eyed tracker who could have followed
Plata's hoofs upon that course from the Ancho road! He
looked out across the miles of sun-flooded hill and plain
and shook his head.

"Lovely, mightily lovely," he said aloud. "I wouldn't
give a hoot for a man who didn't like Texas. This part of it
in particular. Of course—" he grinned sardonically—
"maybe I'm a little more inclined that way, than usual, this
morning. For it could be on the cards easy enough that this
is the last morning I'll ever see the country . . ."

And he kneed Plata into a long, swinging trot.

"Come on, you! Pick up those feet. What're you
waiting on, anyhow? Not expecting to see that Jonas
fellow, I hope? Why, you simple-minded *caballo*, you!
He's not coming. In fact, I doubt if he's been born yet!"

Plata grunted and surged up a scrub-studded comb of the hills. Mechanically Lace stared to the right, along a gash of the lower swells that gave him view of a segment of what Smoky Hills had always called Injun Trail. He pulled Plata in short and stared. Injun Trail, down there, crossed a long meadow, and along it, in single file, men were riding.

He frowned, wondering who used that dim, seldom-traveled road today.

"Nine li'l' dots . . ." he said slowly. "Yes, sir, nine dots. Now which ones of our Valley citizens could those dots stand for? You're absolutely right, horse, absolutely. That could be just about any nine of the bunch we left at the Rock House."

He went on thoughtfully and, when he came to that spot where the Main Drag dipped down into the Valley itself, he rode very alertly, with carbine across his lap. For there were three set places along here where men could overlook the Drag and send a shredding bail of lead into anyone traveling it—while they themselves remained completely sheltered, virtually unseen.

No regular watch was ever kept, in these natural sentry boxes, but any of them might be manned at any time. All of which made travel very interesting for a man who had just seen nine fast-riding horsemen pass below him, going on what must have been an important errand.

But he had passed two of the little forts and was all but on the Valley's edge when a hail came from over him. His head jerked to the side and the carbine was lifting when Curly Camp called him by name, and gave his own. There was no particular emotion in Curly's voice, but when he came scrambling down to the Drag his face showed grim enough.

"Something told me I ought to side you," Curly grunted, without preface. "But being new to the Valley and knowing you wasn't it did seem that maybe my idees wasn't right. How'd you bust loose from your sheriff?"

"*Amor de dios*! Don't tell me that story's already out?" Lace cried amazedly. "Why, I was planning on telling Tull all about it, myself. Where'd you find out?"

"Everybody in the Valley heard about it last night. And I tell you it raised plenty noise. Just about busted up Tull Farris' schemes. It was that dang' Topeka Gates give it away. He got oryide drunk last night. Come staggering into the Rock House and took on some more load. Gano Brown was there, and Chick Haynes, and that Tulsa Jack outfit. Tull was off somewhere. Don't know where, but he hadn't showed up at the Rock House all afternoon. Well, it wasn't like our night in Ancho, with Topeka. He was really drunk and really talking."

He shrugged grimly and began to roll a cigarette. "Gano Brown was talking about some job he'd pulled in Old Mexico and how he'd schemed it. Topeka kept horning into the talk, and Gano told him a couple of times to shut up. Then Topeka burst out with how slick Tull Farris was. Dang' if he didn't spill the story of Tull sending him and Delgado out to kill Dave Crews. And that wouldn't do the idiot, by itself. He told'em all how Tull had rigged the scheme to send you down to Dragoon Head and right into Sheriff Roy Jacks' paws."

"Topeka!" Lace said wonderingly. "Why, Curly, first thing you know you'll make me believe that everything has got its use—even Topekas! What happened when the nitwit let that out?"

"Blazes!" Curly replied simply. "Nothing but blazes.

Gano Brown and Chick Haynes pulled right out of the Valley. They said they had a bellyful of Tull Farris. If he'd cross a man like you, one everybody knew and trusted, he'd cross his own mother. Tull come in and they gave him hell and he denied it all, but nobody believed him. They called him every kind of crook and sneak they could think of, and rode off. I reckon that fella Tom Elton sort of had a notion Tull had schemed something like that. For he was the worst, in telling Tull what he thought. He went with Chick Haynes."

"The two bunches went together, huh? And where'd they hit for?" Lace asked curiously.

"Yeh, together. And they said they was going into Mexico. But they're pretty light on *dinero*. So I reckon they'll zigzag some before they hit the River. How'd you cut stick from this Jacks? My lord! Getting to be a habit with you two."

"It wasn't so hard—the way it happened," Lace said absently, and told the tale very briefly, but without mention of his ride to Pluma. "That was how it was. Now, what's left in the Valley, with Chick and Gano gone?"

"Everybody's gone. Your old friend, Barto Awe, rode in with four men. Maybe that was what kept Tull Farris from having his heart split in the general row. Barto was on his side. Well, after the two bunches left, Tull got Barto and Tulsa together, and the nine of'em rode off to stick up that Schurzman store at Crow Flat."

"Crow Flat! Why—I thought that was just a stall of Tull's to toll me into Roy Jacks' handcuffs. I figured it must be, after I had made up my mind that he'd crossed me."

"No, seems like they've had a man spying around Schurzman's for more,n a week. And he brought the word that it was time to hit their lick. They wanted me to go with 'em, but—"

He laughed and there was genuine amusement upon his round face. Lace waited.

"Oh, I just said I had always run with curly wolves and it would be too much of a change for me to get down on my belly and start siding coyotes that'd turn a good little *buscadero* in to the Law. And I did tell 'em, too, that while I hadn't been long acquainted with you, I'd seen you work in Ancho. So I'd wait and maybe you'd come back bringing this sheriff's store teeth and handcuffs and watch and chain. They—didn't argue . . ."

There was affection in the grin he turned upon Lace—and much of warmth in Lace's face.

"Well, old-timer?" Curly inquired. "And what's next? It does seem to one pore cowboy from the centerfire range that you are kind of riding the critter. For if this Heinie Schurzman kills Barto Awe, that saves us the time and the trouble. And if he happens to get clear of Crow Flat and comes back to the Valley, you'll drill him when he shows up. I reckon, between the two of us, we can see that it's just gun for gun. I can keep that bunch of scabbies he's got from buying in . . ."

"Thanks! That's the way I would like it—just Barto Awe bucking me. I think that lick at Crow Flat is a fool notion. If old Heinie Schurzman didn't spot Tull's man inside of eight hours and sort of fool around until he figured out what was in his mind, then I don't know that Dutchman. He was a scout and a cavalryman too long to be fooled by any but the best. I'm willing to bet the gang goes after gold and brings back lead. If they're able to bring back anything . . ."

"And when all that's settled, how about a little *pasear*

160

down into Mexico with me? You know, fella, the high lines put a mark on you. Once the dog runs with the wolves he's not apt to come back to the ranch and bark at the door. Uh-uh! You tried it. You tried to be an honest nester and as soon as a robbery was pulled inside fifty miles of you, they reached out and hauled you in— and made the thing stick! Well, why not admit you're licked and come along with me. I like your style and I think you like mine. I wouldn't want a better partner . . ."

"Neither would I!" Lace assured him earnestly. "But—oh, I told you the layout. I'm on parole and if I prove that Barto Awe and his bunch pulled the Pluma job, I've got a pardon coming. Even if it is a pardon for something I didn't do, it's a pardon. So I'm bent on delivering Barto Awe to Roy Jacks. I've proved to my own satisfaction that it was Barto in Pluma. After I got loose from Roy in Ancho, I rode over to Pluma and talked to that crooked express clerk, Seth Ramsay—the one Marian told me about. He was the tipper. By this time he ought to be in Pluma jail unloading every thing he ever knew. Maybe the names of Barto Awe's gang. But if he didn't know which gang did the work, what Marian can tell will clinch that."

"You're not figuring on looping Barto Awe and handing him over to a sheriff?" Curly said with slow incredulity.

"In a way. But my way! You're right about one thing, Curly. I'm no regular John Law. I've gone up and down with our kind too long and too far ever to turn bloodhound on'em. You know how I turned down the offer of paroles and pardons until I found out that it was Barto Awe I would have to hunt. That made it a lot different. For I sent word to Barto after he shot Bob

161

Vardon in the back that it would be shoot on sight. And he dang' well never let it come to sight, either!"

He drew a long, slow breath. Curly watched intently the hardening of his friend's bronzed face, the tightening of his wide mouth. Lace beat upon his saddle horn with a big fist.

"I'm after Barto Awe now, and nobody else. I don't have to take orders from anybody. So I can find Barto and give him the even break he wouldn't give anybody, didn't give Bob Vardon. When that time comes, I'm as sure of killing him as I am that we're here on the Main Drag. I'll deliver him to Roy Jacks. I will that! But he'll be a dead man when I do. And when I prove it was Barto that did those Pluma murders, they'll have to admit I filled my end of the contract I made with Judge Bettencourt—even if I filled it according to my own ideas, and never bothered about other Long Riders that Roy Jacks would have corraled. I reckon that's the map."

"Sounds like a good map," Curly grunted. "For a Long Rider turned detective, it sounds like the only map you could use. I tell you what, Lace—when you start down the old Honest Road again, you better study to be a lawyer. Seems to me you're wasting your head, being a dang' nester."

He turned toward the brush that walled in this side of the Main Drag. "I'll get my hawse. He's staked out, hundred yards up the slope yonder. I figured you would come this way, after old Concha told me about these trails up here. That old gal and me, we get along fine. And she thinks a world of you."

He brought back his stocky bay and waited for Lace, who sat Plata scowling uncertainly toward Injun Trail.

"I had figured to go on down into the Valley," Lace

said slowly, "but now, I think we can do better if we trail Barto and Tulsa Jack's bunch. It's a feeling in my bones, sort of."

CHAPTER 22

LACE STARED ALONG THE MAIN DRAG, IN THE direction of the Valley "town." He had intended going on to the Rock House. He felt, somehow, that down there a slim, white-faced girl watched with wide, dark eyes for Lace Morrow's coming. Perhaps, with these sudden shifts and changes in the Valley, Marian Crews needed him. And that thought checked him, made him hesitate.

But he was still more the man riding a bitter enemy's trail than the man in love. He would even argue with himself—he had been arguing with himself—that he was not in love. Lord! He had hardly seen the girl, had talked to her only twice, under her cabin window about her own troubles, and the moment when he had said "*hasta la vista*" to her. A man didn't fall in love with a woman that soon, not a man like Lace Morrow, anyway.

"The squabble has probably made it safer for her," he decided at last. "Tull has got too much on his mind right now to be bothering about women. It's not as if he had been off in the hills a year. He's had all the female society any man needs, all the time, with Bella and that crew of floozies in the dance-hall. Uh-uh! I'm just acting the kid."

But he wondered what she thought of him, this afternoon. A killer, she had termed him at first. Then she seemed to alter her opinion. Perhaps—He asked Curly about her.

163

"Why, she come down to the Rock House kitchen a time or two that I know about. Went on back to her cabin."

"She—she—You figured she was all right?"

"Why—seemed so to me, yeh. You didn't expect Tull to be gobbling her up, or some of the others to grab her?"

Curly's tone was one of surprise, and Lace shook his head and managed a careless manner when he said he was only wondering about her, just happened to think of her.

"Ready to head for Crow Flat?" he asked Curly. "I don't reckon we can land there before Barto's crew has tried a lick at Heinie Schurzman. But we'll see what we can see."

"When I was a kid—" Curly was grinning "—the boys on the XY spread used to say I would leave whisky for a woman and run off from the prettiest woman in the world for a good fight—and never stop to pick up my hat! Let's go!"

They rode down to cut into Injun Trail and pick up the tracks of Barto Awe and his eight followers. They rode fast, but those ahead of them, going toward the store and freight corrals of grim old Heinie Schurzman, had also been traveling at racing gait. At dusk they rested and shared a can of tomatoes Lace had in his saddle bags.

Lace knew this trail very well. He thought it a gamble if Barto Awe would use it on the return trip from Crow Flat. There were other roads he could take. Too, he might find himself so hammered by the Dutchman's men that he would head into the first path that presented itself.

For the first time in several nights, there was a moon.

But the light only seemed to make blacker the trees and brush that walled in the trail. Lace grunted.

"Moonlight's not always the pretty thing the poet tells about," he said. "It does light up the glo-o-rious beauty of Nature and all that, but—"

"—It makes glo-o-rious targets out of us, too!" Curly finished. "Well, it's the chance us young cowboys take."

At midnight they were still short of Crow Flat. The robbery, or the attempt at robbery, should be about over, Lace decided. He wondered if the raiders had used the plan which Tull Farris—feeling secure in his knowledge that Lace would be in jail—had described. Wondered, also, if there was a traitorous clerk to open the door for Barto.

They came up to where the rimrock of the mesa showed overhead. That mesa was Crow Flat. And now they heard shots. . . Curly rode up beside Lace, patting the smooth walnut butt of his Winchester. He leaned forward, plain in the moonlight, a leashed bulldog straining to charge. The firing increased. It was like faraway thunder, swelling to a roar, diminishing, swelling and diminishing again.

"What the blazes's happening up there?" Curly grunted impatiently. "You'd think that after all that powder burning somebody ought to be on the run—one side or the other. Barto couldn't hope to fight all the men you say this Schurzman'd throw out against him, if the Dutchman was expecting a fight. If he didn't hit a surprise lick, if he didn't make his crack at the safe before all that shooting broke out, he's licked and on the run right now. And nobody's come this way, Lace! What do you make of it?"

"If Tull and Barto got themselves out-guessed, and if

old Heinie was looking for this lick at his safe—why, maybe Barto has got himself cut off from the straight trail back to the Valley—this trail. Tell you, Curly. Let's slide around the rim of the mesa and take a look at the Pluma trail that comes across Crow Flat and drops down the hills. But we've got to be careful. For if Heinie got Barto Awe on the run, the men from the stores will hang and rattle to their haunches like a pack of wolves after a deer. And we've got to be sure which outfit we start shooting at. We haven't got any reason to slam lead at Schurzman. What I want is Barto Awe!"

They turned and by narrow, rugged cross-trails circled the rim of Crow Flat. It was hard going, slow. An hour passed and still another. Lace was irritable. The delay chafed him. If Barto had got clear, that meant another chase, and Barto was as slippery as a hunted wolf. And if Heinie Schurzman's man had chanced to kill Barto—.

"Well, my chances of a pardon are going to be pretty skinny," he told himself grimly.

When they reached the Pluma road they found it empty. But Lace swung down and scratched matches in the shelter of his cupped palm. He moved on his knees up the trail, striking match after match. At last he stood up straight and worked his body in a circle.

"Plenty of tracks. Made inside the hour, too, if I'm any guesser. Twelve or fifteen horses, old timer. And, with everything so quiet up above, my guess is that Barto's bunch—what the Schurzman warriors left of it—is on the run down this-here-now road. I don't fancy being around this mesa while Heinie Schurzman is mopping up the scraps. So our best bet looks to be trailing along this way, to find out what's what and who's who."

166

Pluma, by this road, was thirty miles away. They rode at a trot in that direction. And, after a time, Curly swore that he heard shots. Lace was not sure, but they went on more cautiously with their carbines across their arms. Dawn had come before they heard or saw anything else to guide and warn them.

From a brush-crowned hilltop Curly searched the timber beyond with his binoculars. Lace studied the trail. He had an uncanny gift for this business, developed by years with Smoky Hills—who could almost out-trail an Indian. He found the same medley of hoofprints which he had seen below the Flat. But suddenly he grunted inquiry. Curly had called tensely to him.

"Dozen men coming like blazes this way!" Curly explained. "Here, you take the glasses. You know the best people of the neighborhood. You can make out some of the faces."

Lace accepted the binoculars and instantly recognized the wide, hunched figure of Heinie Schurzman at the head of those riders. There was something about the Dutchman that reminded him of a questing hound, hunting trail.

"Let's get out of this and into the timber-fast!" he said to Curly. "That's Schurzman himself and he's looking for the scraps I spoke about. We can get around 'em and go on."

They mounted in the shelter of the rise and went off the road. Lace led the way in a shallow half-circle that brought them back to the trail behind Schurzman's fighting cowboys. And presently they reached the place in the road which explained the storekeeper's wheel about. For all fresh sign ended in the hard trail. Lace looked thoughtfully about him.

167

"Schurzman lost the trail here . . . And I'll bet you a purse of gold against a lock of your golden hair, my son, that I know ex-actly what Barto did. Yes, sir! He cut over the rocks right back yonder a li'l' bitsy piece. He headed for the trails along the Release. And if something hasn't happened to those trails, *I* know 'em a sight better than Barto will live long enough to learn'em. I know one that'll cut off a couple of hours from any they know enough to take. One that runs into the Valley trail that Barto will have to take."

"Think this bullhead' Dutchman is giving up the proposition?" Curly asked him.

"I wouldn't bet you a nickel on it. We've got to be on the lookout every minute. His outfit'll be combing these hills so fine you'd think Barto Awe was gold-plated. And that bunch of his, Curly my young friend, they would perforate our hides just as gay and free as ever they'd blast wicked folk like Barto Awe and his friends from Green River. Put that bunch of wisdom in one of your letters home!"

He led the way through underbrush for a mile, covering that trackless expanse solely by his sense of direction. Then they found a narrow, dim trail, and turned into it. Lace grunted to Plata and sent the big gray forward at a lope.

Mile after mile they rode along this thirty-inch path, with branches banging their booted legs, their arms, their face. And at last they came into another and more-traveled trail, on the Release. But there were no fresh tracks on its floor, and Lace snarled wolfishly at this. Curly Camp's face was no longer good-humored and innocent. One might have thought that he, also, rode the blood trail today. Then both stiffened.

"Coming fast!" Lace said curtly. "If it should be that

trifling dang' bunch from the Green River—"

There was nothing to do but ride out into the trail in the very faces of these harried runaways. For Lace could not bring himself to do the sensible thing and open fire from ambush. But he would not pull Curly into it—

"This is me—all me!" he called savagely. "You stay under cover and let me take the chances—"

He jumped Plata forward. He had one flashing glimpse of Barto Awe's big, well-remembered, utterly-hated figure, in the lead of the riders. Then a snaky little dark man who looked like a breed. And last, the big, red Noisy of Tulsa's bunch. The mixture seemed to prove the completeness of Heinie Schurzman's counter-blow at the outlaws, Lace thought.

Then he was sitting Plata before them. Barto Awe jerked his tall chestnut horse down upon its tail. For an instant he glared with red-tinged black eyes, then—with a yell to those with him—he roweled the chestnut aside, jumping him into the brush. And Noisy was as fast.

But the dark little man was over-warlike. With a sudden snarling flash of teeth, he whipped out a pistol and began to fire. It seemed to Lace that he could hear bullets whining within an inch of his ear. The shots came from his shoulder. And the dark little warrior was coming sideway and forward out of the saddle when Barto and Noisy began to fire from the brush that sheltered them.

Lace spurred Plata hard and the gray horse lunged in a jackrabbit-jump straight into the brush. Lace flung himself out of the saddle and sprawled flat upon the ground with his carbine thrust out ahead.

From somewhere on his right, Curly was shooting thunderously. Reply came from one of the hidden men. The *rap-rap-rap* of bullets upon leaves was an undertone for the roar of rifles and pistols.

Lace began inching toward the man who had shot at Curly. He was afraid in this moment of only one thing—that Barto Awe's well-known discretion would come into play, that Barto would leave Noisy to kill or be killed and he himself slip away, as so evidently he had done at Crow Flat.

Lace moved cautiously, his head shuttling to left and right. Any bush might mask one of the men—that man who was not firing steadily at Curly. Wary as he was, Lace heard nothing at all, saw nothing, until a tiny rustle behind him sent him in a jaguar-leap, straightening quickly, to the side. As he whirled about a pistol roared and a bullet went past too close for comfort.

It was Noisy and, after his shot, be dropped to his knees and went at the oddest gait Lace had ever seen—running backward while squatting, flipping the hammer for another shot. His heavy face was twisted in a venomous mask, made the more sinister by the bloody track of a bullet which had skinned across his cheek—at Crow Flat, doubtless.

Lace pumped .44 slugs at him from the hip, as fast as he could work the carbine lever. Something rapped upon the crown of his hat. Then Noisy seemed suddenly all flexing joints. He fell as if he were boneless, collapsing in a huddle rather than dropping.

A bullet came singing across the little clearing in which they had fought, to thud soggily into a tree. Another followed almost at once and barked a sapling a yard from Lace. He took the hint, and copied that squatting run of Noisy's, to get back into the cover of the brush. He crouched there, glaring toward the place from which Barto Awe's lead had come.

Lace had always owned supreme confidence in his

ability with either Colt or rifle. He had always been sure that, when he faced Barto Awe, the meeting must end with Barto's death. But that did not mean that he discounted the big outlaw's competence with weapons. From the Hole to Cananea, Long Riders knew Barto Awe as a gunman and a killer.

Barto was a cautious soul. He liked the breaks. He would shoot at no man from the front, if it were possible to kill him from behind. And he had a homicidal mania. He liked to kill. Here in this brush, he was more dangerous than a hidden rattlesnake. So Lace set himself for a duel. Characteristically, he forgot Curly, who might surely be expected to help very efficiently and willingly.

He began to circle through the brush, moving soundlessly in spite of high-heeled boots. He heard nothing and when he came to the place where two ejected shells glinted on the ground, nobody was there. He went on, hunting for Barto Awe—who, doubtless, was somewhere beyond and hunting *him*!

Then he straightened, standing behind a bush. He edged around it and—there was Barto Awe, carbine in big, hairy paws, just wheeling to face him. Barto made a harsh, strangling sound, at the sight of Lace. His carbine jumped up like a thing with a murderous soul all its own, eager to kill.

Lace squeezed the trigger of his Winchester and the hammer clicked upon an empty chamber. He dropped it, saving precious time by merely opening his hands. Down to the butt of his Colt his hand dropped—as if in an exhibition of the quick draw . . .

A slug from Barto Awe's carbine seared his left shoulder as the muzzle of his Colt cleared the holster-top. But Lace was concentrated upon one thing and one only—that big figure before him which must be knocked down. In his years of Long Riding, he had needed to face only a few men over cocked guns. His ability at gunplay had made men slow to bring a quarrel to a blazing finale. But he had the gunman's instinct, the way of ignoring everything but the job of drawing, aiming, killing. And so it was, now.

Three times, Barto Awe pressed the trigger of that short Winchester, while Lace was firing at him as fast as he could flip back the hammer and let it drop. But after that first hit upon Lace's shoulder, Barto's lead went to the right and left a trifle. For he was being staggered by heavy bullets, pounding into his body.

Lace shot his pistol empty and let it fall, then reached into his waistband and got out his second gun, before realizing that Barto was not shooting at him. He began to walk toward his enemy, cocked pistol ready. Barto was swaying, the carbine dropping as if suddenly too much of a burden for his hands.

"If I had—got you—wouldn't mind-going!" he said thickly. "If I could have—downed you—"

"Going like Barto Awe!" Lace told him contemptuously. "Lying! You would have minded, no matter who you got. I only wish I could have killed you twice! Curly! Oh, Curly! It's all over now. All over. . .

CHAPTER 23

CURLY CAME OVER TO STAND BESIDE LACE AND LOOK down at the three bodies so conspicuously sprawling in the trail. Lace stared at the bullet wounds in Barto Awe—five shots that might be covered with a man's two palms.

Curly jerked a thumb at the square of brown paper buttoned to Barto's shirt. "You don't want to forget what I told you, about studying for the law when you get back."

"This does kind of roll up the ball of twine," Lace nodded. "With that plain trail you left for old Heinie Schurzman, he'll be up here inside a half-hour or so. And when they find that notice about Barto and the others doing the Pluma killings, I reckon Heinie will be willing to tell Roy Jacks he has got the Pluma gang. He's got the tail-end of the outfit that tried to clean out his safe."

He looked thoughtfully at the little breed, the first man to fall. From this one Curly had got the story of Barto Awe's unlucky blow at Crow Flat, before the little man had died.

They had been expected. They had run into a blast of fire at the corrals. Dynamite and Lanny—who with Tulsa Jack and Noisy had started shooting down the trail to draw Schurzman's men away from the store— had been killed instantly. But Noisy and Tulsa had got away untouched, to find themselves riding with Barto Awe and this little half-Cherokee. But a bullet had knocked Tulsa Jack from the saddle as the quartette turned to gallop away from Crow Flat.

"Well," Lace said slowly, "I reckon we can say that the worst bunch of human wolves that ever rode these parts is a matter of history. Let's go on down to the Valley. Can't be any men there now, but Tull Farris and Topeka, and maybe that Mex' kid who rode down to Roy Jacks with Tull's word about me. Nothing to matter. I'm going to just ride in and tell Tull that I'm taking Marian Crews out of the Valley. I somehow can't see Tull putting up much of an argument . . . ."

"My notion is, Tull won't be arguing about much of anything for a while, after he hears about what happened to Barto Awe and Tulsa Jack," Curly said dryly. "Well, when you've got that pretty bolt of calico under your arm, try to make the wedding somewhere that a man like me can take it in. I wouldn't miss it if I had to buy some new boots to dance in."

"Who said anything about a wedding?" Lace demanded in a surprised voice. "A man like me, getting married! Even if she was willing. She's a nice kid and I'm an old battle-scarred *buscadero* that's just happened to be lucky in this deal."

"I'm glad to hear that," Curly told him solemnly, as they mounted and turned toward the Valley. "I never could figure why anybody would want to get married."

Then he laughed and Lace turned toward him suspiciously.

"Don't try to hoorah me, fella! I've seen your face when you mentioned her. And when your name was spoke in the kitchen at the Rock House, I saw her face. So, when the wedding comes off, I expect to be one of the happy dancers."

They rode fast for a time. For, while it was possible that Heinie Schurzman would be satisfied with sight of those dead robbers, it was also possible that curiosity about the men who had so considerately left Barto Awe in the trail might lead the Dutchman to follow. But after various doublings over rocky ground they relaxed their gait. Lace had time to think. And he found himself thinking of Marian Crews.

She's pretty—if you don't expect floozie-prettiness. A nice kid every way you can think of. And she has got under my skin . . . Nobody else ever made me feel just this way. But that's only part of it. I'm a tough character. When she gets out of the Valley and among ordinary people, how's she going to feel about me? I was the only one she could turn to here. Probably seemed a lot better than I am, because I was the one who didn't make grabs at her. But outside—I don't know . . .

Back to the Valley they came, and past that place where Curly had waited for Lace. Everywhere there was quiet. Not that much noise ever disturbed Lost Souls Valley, except around the Rock House. But it was a relief to Lace to come in sight of the straggling line of cabins and see smoke curling blue and lazy from a chimney or two. He sighed.

"Let's tear down and kind of catch Tull off his guard! We're bringing the sad news about Crow Flat to him."

So they raced down the Valley and the thudding drum of the hoofs drew a girl or two to door or window. But they rode on with no more than glances at these staring faces. Before the Rock House they pulled in to a sliding stop and let the split-reins drop. Inside the bar-room they ran and stood staring around. Ike was not behind the bar. The room was empty.

"Funny!" Lace grunted. "Wonder where he went?"

Then Topeka Gates appeared, standing as if drunk in the door of the back room.

"Where's Tull?" Lace demanded. "Talk up, you!"

Topeka shambled a step into the bar-room and indicated with a jerk of the head the room he had left. Lace watched him suspiciously as he walked toward the door. But Topeka reeked of liquor. Lace went on into the other room.

There was a bundle in a corner and from it came gasping noises. Lace went like a cat toward it and stooped. Then, without a sound to warn him, he found himself gripped, body and neck, by long, steely arms.

He had thought himself a powerful man, but Topeka lifted him from the floor and held him helpless. The tall man's arms threatened to crack his ribs, paralyze his gunarm. He sagged and Topeka flung him to the floor.

Lace held himself moveless. He watched Topeka, who stood with head rolling from him to that sack-swathed figure in the corner. He wondered if he could get a gun out with his left hand. Then Topeka stepped back deliberately. He fumbled behind him and dragged a double-bitted axe out into sight. He lurched out with a speed Lace had never expected from that shambling body. The axe lifted and descended and Lace rolled desperately away. That glinting blade buried itself almost to the handle-hole in the floor, so close to Lace's shoulder he thought himself struck.

A Colt bellowed somewhere as Topeka strained to free the axe, bellowed again and again. Topeka began to bend. His head sagged forward, his shoulders drooped, his knees buckled. He fell like a grotesque toy, broken. Lace sat up and faced Curly, walking into the room with gray smoke rising from his Colt muzzle.

"Good boy!" he thanked him wheezily. "See who that is."

Curly came past him and began to tug at the lashings on the woman—for it was a woman. When he jerked off the sack Bella-wild-eyed, haggard, furious—sat up. She was gagged, and when Curly took out the wadded bandanna from her mouth she swore viciously. Lace, recovered now from the anaconda-grip, stepped toward her with a snarl that stopped her short.

"Where's Tull?" he asked her. "Cut out the noise! Nobody is interested but you. Where is he?"

"Where do you think he'd be? Down at Marian's

cabin, of course! When he heard about Crow Flat he went wild! Scared that crazy Dutchman'd be here next. So he knocked me out and tied me up and he's gone—"

Lace did not wait for more. He ran for the back door and was hardly outside when he heard the noise from Marian Crews' cabin down the line. From the sound, everything breakable in the place was being smashed.

He ran up the slope and threw himself at the door. It was barred, and he backed off, breathing heavily, hardly conscious of anything but the barrier that held him back. Then the dull explosion of a shot inside was followed by the tearing noise of a bullet coming through that door. Another shot brought another slug past him.

There was nothing with which he might batter down that door—nothing but his own heavy shoulder. He threw himself against the door and it quivered in the frame—but held. And now the girl's thin scream carried to him, cutting through other sounds like a knife.

"Lace! Lace! He'll kill you!"

Bullet after bullet crashed through the heavy planks as he threw himself at the door. Tull Farris, it would seem, was trying to locate him by altering aim. The slugs came high and low and through the center of the door. Lace stepped back again and shook his head in a bull-like motion. A sort of haze floated before his eyes. He went around the cabin and found all the windows shuttered. At the end he stopped.

"Chimney!" he said to himself, chokingly. "Chimney. . ."

He ripped the cartridge belt from his waist with a jerk at the strap-end, let the burden fall. Then he walked backward three steps. He ran forward and jumped, twisting sideway as his fingertips caught the eaves. He swung up and crouched on the roof. It was hard to hold

177

his balance on those sun-dried shakes, but he worked upward until he was at the chimney.

It was a huge affair, built of rough field stones. He scrambled to its top, then let himself down into it, heedless of the sharp points of rock and mortar. He was gashed and bruised as he dropped its height and landed with a crash on the wide stone hearth.

Tull Farris turned at the door with a yell. He lifted his pistol as Lace crouched and hinged toward him. Lace heard the roar of the shot, heard the bullet strike somewhere. But he ran at the tall king of the Valley, a terrible figure, blood-soaked, soot-blackened, big hands out . . .

Tull's hammer clicked upon an empty cylinder. Then he struck viciously at Lace with the long barrel of his pistol. Lace swung to the side, and the pistol no more than grazed him. He caught Tull Farris by the throat with his left hand and drove heavy blows to the body with his right. Tull dropped the pistol and Lace caught him suddenly with both hands about the waist. He heaved and Tull Farris came up to hurtle over his shoulder and crash into the wall. When he whirled about, Tull Farris lay motionless with head turned at an unnatural angle to his body.

Dazedly, he looked about him. The rough plank table and the benches were overturned. The floor was a litter of bright blankets and pots and pans and heavy dishes. In a corner, face like a torn bit of white paper, Marian Crews was huddled. Lace went to her and stood panting.

"*Querida!*" he said thickly. "I—I must've gone crazy. I wouldn't let that snake put his hands on you—You hurt? Tell me! Did he hurt you, even a little bit?"

She opened her eyes and stared at him fearfully. Then she slumped and closed them again. Her lips moved faintly. "I kept saying it—saying it to myself—while I ran from him and fought with him. If only I could keep him from getting me—for just a little while longer— you'd be here!"

She turned and began to pull herself up. Lace reached to catch her arms and draw her against him.

"I knew you'd come," she whispered. "You said you'd be here when I needed you. I knew you'd come here and kill him. But—I didn't know whether you could get here in time—"

She put her hand weakly to her eyes and he held her closer against his shoulder. She turned a little in his arms and let her head go back so that she looked up at him.

"It's all right, now," he told her. "Everything's all right. The Valley's cleaned up. Barto Awe and all the killers are finished. Come over here and sit down, *querida.*"

She moved with him to a bench and sat down beside him. But when she found the blood soaking his sleeve, from one of Tull Farris' bullets, she cried out and stiffened. "You're hurt! He hit you! We'll have to bandage that!"

"It's nothing. Nothing at all. Just a nick one of his slugs made coming through the door. And you're— everything. Funny . . . I don't know why you're so important. This makes the fourth time I've seen you. But you're the big thing. I'm going to take you away from here. You'll never see, or hear about any of this again. I'm going to take you away with me."

"Of course! You have to take me. I won't stay behind. I want to go with you wherever you go. If you have to dodge officers, I'll dodge them with you. If you want to leave Texas and go to Mexico, we'll go together. I can ride. I haven't a soul in the world, now, but you. And from the first time I saw you, I knew there was nobody like you. But—you didn't even look at me that first time . . ."

Her arms came up around his neck, and she clung to him like a frightened child. Yet—not altogether like a child, either . . . . In her face was that something which told him that she was not a girl, now, but a woman. And the tightening of her arms told whose woman. He lifted her chin with a big hand.

"You—you really mean that you'll go with me—the kind of man I am—time without end and—"

"And beyond that! I'll go with you always. As long as you want me. And—and if you decided that you didn't want me any longer I—probably I'd be like poor Bella, about Tull; I'd try to kill the woman you did want!"

"Then I reckon we won't do any dodging, *querida mia*. We don't need to. I've got a parole down in Pluma, this minute. And by the time we get there it ought to have blossomed out into a full-sized pardon. We'll ride down to Pluma and hunt up Judge Bettencourt. He's a district judge. And if he charges for marrying us, I swear I'll rob his house to pay the charge. Then we'll start out as an honest nester family. For we're done with the high lines, *querida*. Done with Long Riders."

Curly's voice lifted outside. Lace thought that he had been hearing it for minutes, now. He got up and went over to throw the bar of that bullet-shredded door. Curly came in, to look quickly and shrewdly around. Finding Tull Farris he nodded and came across to where Lace sat beside Marian.

"Well, I reckon that kind of settles the cat-hop," he said. "And I suppose you'll be riding down to Pluma

180

when you have got yourself sort of decent. Uh—
Lace . . . You're not forgetting what I told you about
having that wedding after dark? Because I'm not sure
about showing myself in a judge's house in daylight.
And I certainly intend to be one of the dancers at this
wedding, before I hightail it for Mexico . . . "

"Ten o'clock tomorrow night!" Lace told him, and
grinned. "That'll give you all the dancing you can
handle and still you can be on the old Bravo Trail by
daylight! Let's go . . ."

We hope that you enjoyed reading this
Sagebrush Large Print Western.
If you would like to read more Sagebrush titles,
ask your librarian or contact the Publishers:

United States and Canada

Thomas T. Beeler, *Publisher*
Post Office Box 659
Hampton Falls, New Hampshire 03844-0659
(800) 818-7574

United Kingdom, Eire, and
the Republic of South Africa

Isis Publishing Ltd
7 Centremead
Osney Mead
Oxford OX2 0ES England
(01865) 250333

Australia and New Zealand

Bolinda Publishing Pty. Ltd.
17 Mohr Street
Tullamarine, 3043, Victoria, Australia
(016103) 9338 0666